★ ───────

LaRoche's body must have been under the table—there were no two ways about it.

It stood to reason that the table had been placed over him where he had fallen. Otherwise, there would have been blood somewhere else in the room, and I certainly hadn't seen any. There had been the spot that Sarah and I were trying to cover when we moved the table the next morning, but that definitely was not blood.

No, I was fairly certain LaRoche was already under the table.

Then there was the other million-dollar question: why hadn't I noticed something was wrong? The murder weapon was sitting in a ring of blood. There was a body under the table, for God's sake. How could I have missed it all?

The answer was obvious. I'd had three or four glasses of wine in the bar. I was drunk. I didn't know which was scarier—that I was drunk enough not to notice a dead man, or that I had been drunk enough not to notice a dead man *and* I had driven home.

───────── ★ ─────────

Previously published Worldwide Mystery title by
SANDRA BALZO

UNCOMMON GROUNDS

Sandra Balzo

GROUNDS
FOR
MURDER

a Maggy Thorsen mystery

WORLDWIDE.

TORONTO • NEW YORK • LONDON
AMSTERDAM • PARIS • SYDNEY • HAMBURG
STOCKHOLM • ATHENS • TOKYO • MILAN
MADRID • WARSAW • BUDAPEST • AUCKLAND

Recycling programs
for this product may
not exist in your area.

GROUNDS FOR MURDER

A Worldwide Mystery/June 2010

First published by Severn House.

ISBN-13: 978-0-373-26711-8

Printed in U.S.A.

GROUNDS
FOR
MURDER

ONE

'SLUT IN A CUP!'

It might sound like an expletive, but my friend Sarah Kingston meant… Well, I wasn't sure what she meant.

'Are you nuts?' I hissed. 'It's Marvin LaRoche. And he's dead.'

I was trying to keep my voice down in an effort to appear calm. The packed bleachers in front of us held nearly two hundred spectators, all of them staring openmouthed at us, like we were actors on a stage. Which we were.

Sarah and I stood stage right, holding up opposite ends of the table bearing the trophies for the Second Annual Barista Competition at Java Ho, the specialty coffee convention. A barista is the equivalent of a coffee bartender, with espresso taking the place of alcohol.

The audience had probably assumed we were shifting the table in preparation for the awards ceremony that would follow the morning's finals. The truth was, though, I'd found an oval stain smack dab in the middle of the stage and—obsessive personality that I am—I had to camouflage it.

Putting the trophy table, with its floor-length white tablecloth, over the stain had seemed just the thing.

Unfortunately, when we'd lifted the table from its original position, we revealed something nobody could cover up.

Marvin LaRoche, head judge and Java Ho organizer, was lying faceup, his burgundy tie flipped over his shoulder. The man was slightly cross-eyed in life, and now his blue eyes seemed to be trying to get a good look at the two bloody dents in his own forehead.

I shivered.

Sarah glared at me. 'I know who it is, Maggy, and even *I* can tell he's dead.'

She'd been in a vile mood ever since I'd commandeered her from the exhibit hall to track down LaRoche for the finals. You'd think she'd be happy now that we'd found him.

Sarah nodded toward the biggest trophy, which had fallen over when we'd picked up the table. 'I'm talking about the murder weapon.' She dropped her end, and the smaller runner-up trophies toppled over even as the first-place prize began to slide.

'Dammit, Sarah…' I protested, like it really mattered at this point. I mean, stiff on the floor trumps statues on the table, right? Nonetheless, I dropped my end, too, and instinctively grabbed for the trophy. I had to lean across the table, propping myself on my left hand to catch with the right.

'Got it,' I said triumphantly, straightening up with the trophy. Feeling something sticky on my left hand, I looked down at the table where it had been standing.

The trophy, when it had fallen over, had left a thick ring on the tablecloth—the kind a wineglass might make if it had been overfilled. With red wine. *Thick* red wine.

And that wasn't the only thing being thick. Now I *finally* understood what Sarah had meant.

I looked again at LaRoche on the floor and then back at the barista competition's first-place trophy in my hand. Slut in a cup, as Sarah had called it.

The fifteen-inch bronze sculpture was an artist's rendering of a barista rising like steam from a coffee cup. Since *baristi* come in both genders and all shapes and sizes, the trophy's steamy barista was supposed to be generic. Unfortunately, the unisex steam-barista had… well, boobs. C-cups, if I was any judge. Since it had been too late to do anything about the mistake by the time it was discovered, I'd resigned myself to taking some flak over it.

Still, I hadn't expected anyone to try to bury the boobs in Marvin LaRoche's forehead.

The faintest of tinkling sounded behind me, the only noise in the stunned silence. I twisted around to see the six barista finalists huddled behind us. One was Janalee, LaRoche's wife. She was holding their infant son, Davy, and looking dazed. Next to Janalee was LaRoche's star barista, Amy. In contrast to Janalee's stillness, Amy's multiple piercings—six thin gold rings lining the rim of her right ear, three the left and two in her lips— were quivering so hard she sounded like a human wind chime.

As if on cue, the baby started to whimper and Janalee LaRoche began to scream.

The commotion was enough to make Kate McNamara, newspaper editor-cum-cable-access TV reporter, abandon lecturing her young camera operator and finally take notice of what was going on.

Galvanized, as any good former public relations practitioner would be, by the TV camera now being leveled in my direction, I looked out at the hushed crowd in the bleachers. No one had so much as pulled out a cellphone to call for help. A couple, though, were using theirs to take photos.

I sighed. Apparently, since I, Maggy Thorsen, was in charge of the barista competition, I was also the go-to gal for corpses.

'Call 911,' I said, a familiar chill crawling up my spine.

This was all Caron's fault. Again.

Why—oh, why—hadn't I just said no…?

TWO

'No,' I SAID.

'But you would be perfect, Maggy,' my partner, Caron Egan, had said four days earlier, as she scooped espresso beans into the cone grinder at our coffeehouse, Uncommon Grounds. 'And it's our responsibility to make sure Java Ho is a success.'

It was September, and September meant Java Ho, the specialty coffee tradeshow. The event featured items for the upcoming Christmas holidays, hence the 'Ho' part. Being a latecomer to specialty coffee—Uncommon Grounds having been open only about six months—I didn't have the historical perspective to say whether the convention had once been called Java Ho Ho.

I sincerely hoped not.

Caron was still talking. 'We *are* the host city, after all.'

'No, we're not,' I said. 'The convention center just happens to border on Brookhills.'

Our town chairman, Rudy Fischer, had been apoplectic when the facility was built so near our fashionable little suburb. He said it would draw 'undesirables'. In Brookhills, that meant anyone who didn't drive a BMW.

'Let someone from Milwaukee manage the convention,' I said, wanting the discussion over. 'Besides, if you think it's so important, *you* do it.'

She ignored that. 'Someone from Milwaukee *is* doing most of it.' She put the lid on the cone grinder. 'Marvin LaRoche. He just needs someone to oversee the actual—' I reached across and started the grinder, drowning her out. Caron switched it off and glared at me. 'Barista competition.'

Marvin LaRoche was the owner of HotWired, a chain of coffeehouses that dominated the area. It didn't surprise me that he was taking a very visible role in the specialty-coffee convention.

'I'm sure LaRoche would love to let me do the work,' I agreed. 'Then all he has to do is show up at the finals and take the credit.' I shook my head. 'I've worked with too many grandstanders like him. You did, too, back at the bank.'

At one time, Caron had been in public relations with me at First National Bank. That was years before I, in one fell swoop, lost my son to college, my dentist husband to his twenty-four-year-old hygienist and my job to…well, insanity.

In a knee-jerk reaction to Ted dumping me on the same day our son left for college, I had promptly quit my salaried PR position in order to open Uncommon Grounds with two friends and the proceeds from the sale of Ted's boat.

That'd show him, right?

Wrong.

As I should have guessed, with Miss Rinse-and-Spit to occupy his time, Ted barely noticed the loss of either me *or* his 425-horsepower phallic symbol.

But if one good thing came out of all this, it was the realization that I didn't miss Ted, either. No, it was my *salary* I missed.

You see, I'd morphed into a small-business owner and, as anyone could have told me had I surfaced from my entrepreneurial delusions long enough to listen, small-business owners endure low pay, high pressure and long, *long* hours. Especially when you're one small coffeehouse fighting to stay afloat amidst a sea of chain operations like the one Marvin LaRoche oversaw. *And* when you're one partner light—that partner having been found dead in a pool of nonfat milk the morning we opened.

Guess you could add a partner and a friend to that list of things I'd managed to lose over the last year.

A walking, talking Bermuda Triangle, that's what I was.

Caron was giving me the eye, and it took me a second to realize we were still on the subject of LaRoche. 'It's pronounced La-Ro-Shay,' she said.

'Tell that to his sister Patti.'

I'd gone to high school with Marvin LaRoche's younger sister, and she and the rest of the family pro- nounced their last name La-Roach. Like the bug. Which I thought was appropriate for Marvin, if not for poor Patti. In fact, given Brother Marvin's modus operandi of attaching himself to a person and then sucking the lifeblood out of her, La-Leech would have suited him even better.

The doorbell on our service entrance rang and, happy for an excuse to end the conversation, I started back to answer it. I just hoped it wasn't anyone who expected to be paid.

Caron called after me. 'Most of the planning has been done.'

Sure. The bell chimed again before I could reach it. 'I'm coming!' I said as I pulled open the heavy door. Waiting on the other side was Antonio Silva, owner of The Milkman, the local dairy.

'The Milkman always rings twice,' I said, stepping aside to let him in.

'Ronnie, he rings the bell too much?' Antonio asked with a polite smile. Ronnie was our regular delivery man. 'You prefer, perhaps, that he knock?'

'No, no, not at all,' I hastened to assure him. 'It was just a joke. A pun really.'

Antonio still looked confused.

'*The Postman Always Rings Twice* is a classic American movie,' I explained. 'I can understand why you, being born in Italy, wouldn't have heard of it. It hasn't even been *re*made in more than twenty-five years.'

'And there is a milkman, too, in this movie?' Antonio asked as he thud-thudded the cart laden with milk crates over the wooden threshold. 'In addition to the postman?'

'Yes. I mean, no.' Now I was confusing even myself. 'I just changed the *post*man to a *milk*man because I thought it would be funny.' Thought. As in the past tense.

'Of course. I understand now.' Antonio gave a well-mannered laugh. The kind you save for small children who tell knock-knock jokes.

'Perhaps I should see this movie you are talking about,' he continued. 'Maybe I could make a commercial, using this postman/milkman. Like in the advertisements where the dead movie star dances with the vacuum cleaner?'

'Fred Astaire,' I said automatically. 'But in this case, there really is no postman—'

'There is no postman in *The Postman Always Rings Twice?*' Antonio interrupted.

'No. See the postman in the movie is really a metaphor for justice. Or God. Or fate.' Circle one. 'The allusion is that the bad guys will pay. Even if not right away.'

'On the first ring,' Antonio said, understanding. 'This movie, you are sure it is not Swedish?'

'It *is* of the life-sucks-and-then-you-die variety,' I admitted. 'But it's a great one.'

'I will rent the DVD,' Antonio promised. 'And I will tell Ronnie to ring the buzzer twice from now on. It will be our…how you say it, shtick?'

'Perfect,' I said, with a grin. The man was not only gorgeous, but he was smart and funny in three languages.

'Where *is* Ronnie?' I asked.

'On his vacation,' Antonio said. 'I thought I would deliver myself. So I could catch up with everyone before the coffee convention.'

'Are you going to Java Ho, Antonio?' Caron asked, sticking her head around the corner. 'Marvin LaRoche wants Maggy to oversee the barista competition.'

'Only so he can torture me, up-close and personal.'
Marvin LaRoche and I had a love/hate relationship. I hated
him, and he loved that. Why was Caron pushing this?

'The barista competition is the highlight of the convention,' Antonio said as he squeezed by me in the narrow hall. The refrigerator was wedged next to the desk
in the corner of our office, which also doubled as a
storeroom. 'The Milkman will donate all of the milk
for it.'

Because we used *Antonio* and *The Milkman* in-
terchangeably to refer to the man, it always sounded
like Antonio was talking about himself in charming,
accented third-person when he referred to his dairy.
Combine that with the wavy dark hair, brown eyes and
muscular build and he could slide his carton into my
fridge anytime he wanted.

'It will be excellent visibility, I believe, for anyone
involved,' Antonio said.

There he had a point.

I'd attended my first Java Ho last year, when my
partners and I began toying with the idea of opening a
coffeehouse. Intent on learning the trade and networking, I'd visited all the booths, OD'd on free lattes and
smoothies and completely ignored the hoots and hollers
coming from the barista competition in the next hall.

Ignored, that is, until the last day, when I wandered
into the finals and promptly got hooked on the caffeine-
hyped atmosphere. It was like the World Series, except
with frothing wands instead of bats.

While making specialty coffee drinks might seem simple—throw some ground beans in a filter, push a button, steam some milk—it really can be an art in the right hands. Mine, sadly, are the wrong ones.

A good espresso starts with the proper grind: not too fine and not too coarse. Then just the right amount of pressure applied when tamping, or pressing down the espresso. And a properly timed shot, with the hot water passing through the fine grounds at exactly the right pace and temperature.

Then there was Antonio's department: the dairy products. Whole milk, skim or two-percent. Cream, half-and-half, soymilk, even eggnog for the holidays. All of them are steamed to varying degrees of both heat and frothiness and combined with espresso to make cappuccinos, lattes and other specialty drinks.

The froth itself is important, too. Good froth is almost silky and creative baristas use it and the *crema*—that's the brown foam that comes from brewing espresso—to make intricate, two-tone 'latte art' on top of the drinks.

The key word, of course, being *creative*. The best I'd ever been able to summon up was something that looked like a half-baked version of Princess Leia's hologram in the first *Star Wars* movie. *Help me, Obi-Wan Kenobi...*

'It's really nice of you to donate, Antonio,' Caron was saying, having abandoned the cone grinder to watch him heft six gallons of skim milk, four of whole, and six quarts of half-and-half into our refrigerator.

'There is nothing *nice* about it,' The Milkman said, straightening up and flashing Caron a smile. 'Specialty coffee is of importance to the dairy industry.'

Caron giggled, the trollop.

As Antonio backed into the hall, I dodged out of the way before he could flatten me against the opposite wall. Guys as ripped as Antonio should come equipped with back-up beepers and warning lights.

'Can you imagine how much milk a national chain such as Starbucks purchases each year?' Antonio continued.

I couldn't, but it had to be significant. Uncommon Grounds used a lot of milk and we sure weren't Starbucks, or even LaRoche's HotWired. What Antonio had just loaded into our refrigerator would last us three or four days. We didn't have enough room to stock a full week's supply, so The Milkman delivered on Tuesdays and again Fridays.

'So, what you're saying,' Caron said, wrinkling her pert little nose at Antonio, while simultaneously quirking an eyebrow at me, 'is that you value the exposure.'

The wrinkling-nose/quirking-eyebrow thing seemed physically impossible to me, but then Caron could also touch her nose with her tongue. Eat crackers and whistle. Wiggle her ears. She was a facial Harry Houdini.

'The Java Ho attendees might be potential customers for Antonio,' I pointed out to Caron, 'but they're our competitors. Other coffeehouse owners. Why do we need exposure to them?'

'Two *thousand* coffeehouse owners.' Antonio was obviously delighted at the thought. 'To know who is who and to work into the...how they say it? Rotation of suppliers? Three years to learn this. It will be worth it, though, if I have one more chain like HotWired as my customer.'

'Marvin LaRoche buys milk from you?' I asked. Five years ago, LaRoche had been a barista at Janalee's Place, a small coffeehouse on the northern fringe of Brookhills. Since LaRoche and Janalee had married, the operation had grown to twenty stores.

In fact, the newest HotWired had just opened a bare half-mile from Uncommon Grounds. *Of all the joe joints in all the towns, in all the world...*

'He does,' Antonio was saying. 'And the larger Hot-Wired grows, the more...' He stopped, catching sight of the look on my face.

Caron jumped in. 'Would you like a latte or cappuccino to take along, Antonio?'

'I cannot drink lattes or cappuccinos—thank you.'

'No? Why?' Caron seemed determined to move the subject off HotWired and on to anything else, including Antonio's beverage of choice, apparently.

The Milkman put his hand on his rock-hard abs. Or so I imagined them to be. 'I do not drink the dairy.'

'Wait a second,' I said, being drawn in against my will. 'The Milkman doesn't drink milk?'

Antonio got an embarrassed grin on his face. 'It gives me the stomachache.'

This was just too good.

Leave it to Caron to ruin it for me. 'I understand L'Café is lending the competition three new espresso machines,' she said, back on the attack. 'Everyone sees the potential, Maggy. Even Sarah. She's been coordinating the exhibit hall.'

Sarah Kingston was Brookhills' top real estate agent, and about as unBrookhillian as one could get. She wore baggy jackets on her lean frame, sensible shoes on her oversized feet, and a Virginia Slims Menthol between her tobacco-stained fingers.

In other words, Sarah chain-smoked. Except in her own house, since she was now the guardian of two children. Sarah was considerate of *their* lungs, but hers—and the rest of ours—didn't seem to matter very much.

While Caron might be both my business partner and my oldest friend, Sarah was probably my closest. Caron, despite being a terrible flirt, had that happy-marriage vibe going with her husband, Bernie. While I loved both Caron and Bernie, these days they made me want to hurl—as my son Eric would say.

Yeah, I know. Sour grapes. Or, in my case, crushed, fermented and bottled. The only relationship in my life right now was with red wine. Red didn't mind if I got home at eight thirty or nine at night and cried over a juicy old movie until I fell asleep on the couch. While wine might be impudent, it was seldom snarky or demanding. A little spice, a fair amount of oak and the best of them get better with age. What more could a woman want from a beau?

Except maybe to get corked occasionally.

I'd been hoping for a more…animate lover when I'd met Brookhills County Sheriff Jake Pavlik. Currently, though, we were facing *date-us interruptus,* a condition brought on by fifteen-hour days on my part and an unpredictable schedule on Pavlik's. The fact that I still call him by his last name is an indication of the level of intimacy we've achieved.

Which was yet another reason I couldn't, *wouldn't* devote time to Java Ho. Any free moment I had, I planned to devote to becoming a ho myself.

Antonio slipped out the backdoor with a *ciao* as the bell on the front chimed. Anxious to avoid further nagging from Caron, I fled out into the store to greet the customer, who apparently was hacking up a lung.

I had the cough pegged before I rounded the corner. 'Sarah, you sound awful.' I waved at the cigarette in her hand. 'And put that thing away. You know you can't smoke in here.'

Uncharacteristically, Sarah did exactly what I said. Mid-drag, she took the cigarette out of her mouth and plopped it in her jacket pocket.

'Are you crazy?' I tried to pat her pocket down.

Sarah laughed, which was even more frightening than the spontaneous human combustion I feared. My friend has huge teeth, but not the big 'look-at-me' choppers of actresses and actors. Unless the actor was Mr Ed.

'Gotcha,' she said, pulling the cigarette out and waving it under my nose.

I sniffed. 'It's not lighted. But I could have sworn you were inhaling.'

'Who do you think I am, Bill Clinton? Of course, I inhaled.'

I grabbed the cigarette. 'Hey, this isn't a…' I stopped as a thought struck me. 'This is one of those nicotine inhalers, isn't it? Are you quitting?' I didn't add the word 'again'. It seemed petty. God forbid I should be petty.

'Again?' Caron called from the back.

Ahh. All the satisfaction with none of the guilt.

'Yup.' Sarah pulled a chair away from one of the café tables and turned it around to straddle it. 'But this baby is going to do the trick.'

I examined the white plastic cylinder. 'So, how does it work?' I asked. 'Is it different from the nicotine patch or the gum?'

Sarah took it from me. 'This end of the puffer is really a nicotine cartridge. I inhale nicotine, but much less than I would smoking a cigarette.'

'And "less" is enough to keep you sane?' I was trying not to sound skeptical, but I'd already seen Sarah through four hours of cold turkey, three days of the patch, two weeks of the gum and one really embarrassing hour of hypnotic suggestion.

She took a drag. 'Are you kidding? They want me to use sixteen cartridges a day to start out and each cartridge lasts twenty minutes. That's over five hours of puffing, which pretty much gives me all the oral fix that I need.' She bared her teeth and snickered.

There was some sense to what she was saying, though.

I'd smoked for a short time in my early twenties and, when I'd quit, I'd missed the 'act' of smoking even more than those tasty toxic chemicals. Smoking gives you something to do when your dinner date stands you up, or arrives half an hour late, or picks his nose. Plus, if worst came to worst, you could set him on fire.

Of course, that was back in the days when you could smoke in restaurants. What did people do now to kill time and the occasional bad date?

Cellphones and text-messaging, naturally—at least for the first. The addictions of a new generation. But I mentally digress.

'...convention center is non-smoking, so I figure this should get me through Java Ho,' Sarah was saying.

I tried to regain the ground I'd lost. Or missed. 'So you really *are* running the exhibit hall?'

Caron's voice: 'I *told* you.'

I turned to Sarah. 'But why take on such a huge headache? The exhibit hall at a coffee convention has to have hundreds of suppliers, each one of them vying for the best space.'

'So? Let them vie.' Sarah took a drag and blew make-believe smoke up to the ceiling. 'Inside or outside, it's still real estate.'

'Location, location, location,' Caron offered from the back.

Shaddup, shaddup, shaddup.

'Exactly.' Sarah laughed. 'Except in this case, I can tell them where to go.'

'So you vent your nicotine rage on the Java Ho vendors, instead of your clients.' Now *that* made sense, knowing Sarah.

'If I scream obscenities at a bunch of coffee roasters and frappa-whatever-makers, it doesn't cost me thousands in commissions,' Sarah agreed. 'Besides, I owe LaRoche. He's bought a lot of property through me.'

Didn't I know it. 'Like the spot where the new Hot-Wired is located?'

'We've been through this, Maggy. Business is business.' Sarah shrugged and took a deep drag, turning a little purple in the process. 'Another real estate agent comes in here, are you telling me you won't sell him coffee?'

'That's different and you know it.'

Sarah puffed again. 'You get paid when you sell coffee. I get paid when I sell property. You tell me what's different.'

'Because I'm not...' I started, then clamped my mouth closed. Sarah's biggest competition, Rasmussen Realty, was one of our best corporate clients. We regularly supplied coffee for their meetings and 'Welcome Home' gift baskets for their clients when they moved into their new houses. Rasmussen brokers were in and out of Uncommon Grounds on a daily basis. I guess one could argue that we were fueling them to outsell Sarah.

If one were an idiot.

Caron stuck her head around the corner. 'Sarah, can I make you the usual?'

Sarah nodded. We both kept our mouths shut as my partner positioned the basket of our long-handled portafilter under the cone grinder. She pulled the lever twice, releasing a measured amount of espresso into the filter basket for Sarah's latte.

'You could have warned us at least,' I muttered, not taking my eyes off Caron.

'I may not be a lawyer, or a doctor, or a priest,' Sarah said, 'but I *do* have to maintain confidentiality. I couldn't say anything until the sale of the property to LaRoche was made public. By *him*.' She took a deep drag on her nicotine inhaler. Then another.

Caron had steamed the skim milk and set aside the pitcher. Now she twisted the porta-filter onto the espresso machine and pushed a button.

Yet another drag from Sarah. She was going to asphyxiate herself.

I sighed. 'OK, so you couldn't tell me, what with the Real Estate Brokers' Code of Ethics and all.' Probably right there on the shelf next to Robert's Rules of Used Car Salesmanship.

I hesitated. 'But how long did you know—"

'Lay off, Thorsen,' Sarah snarled. 'Do you want to do this convention or not? It'll be fun. Shit or get off the commode.'

Well, she sure was making it *sound* like fun.

The espresso started to gurgle down through the filter into the miniature metal pitcher Caron had positioned below it and I glanced up at the clock to time the shot. Ten seconds. Too fast.

Before Caron could pour it into Sarah's mug, I reached over and dumped the espresso down the drain. Quality control.

'Short shot,' I snapped. 'You can't serve that.'

OK, so I was ornery. Caron, trying to coerce me into running LaRoche's barista competition. Antonio, cozying up to LaRoche and his HotWired stores. And now Sarah—not only aiding the man's expansion of his evil coffee empire, but running Java Ho's exhibit hall. Was that a giant sucking-up noise I heard?

Instead of getting angry at my shot interference, Caron smiled sweetly at me. 'See? You're a natural espresso Nazi, no matter what you think. You have to run the barista competition.'

'I can't.' Time to backpedal. 'You need me here.'

Sarah grinned. 'Caron can handle it, Maggy. And Courtney and Sam will help.'

Courtney and Sam were Sarah's teenage charges. I was being manipulated by a master, I realized. By *two* masters. What I didn't know was why.

I was about to find out.

Caron said, 'That would be great. One thing, though—' her smile grew wider as she turned to me— 'while you're there, Maggy, I need you to steal us a barista.'

'To steal a…?'

'Specifically, I need you to steal *Amy*.'

THREE

AMY.

The name struck fear within competitive barista circles.

I have a tendency to underestimate Caron in things commercial. She's been out of the corporate world for nearly two decades, having decided to stay home when her son, Nicky, was born. I'd continued to work after having Eric, in part because I loved what I did, but also because Ted was just getting his dental practice up and running and we needed the money.

This was after I'd put him through dental school, of course. Not that I'd minded. It was for our future, after all. Little did I know that 'our' future would turn out to be a ménage à trois, with me the trois. Twit.

I'd caught glimpses of Ted and his bit of floss playing tennis at the Brookhills Racquet Club on my way home from Uncommon Grounds recently. My ex-husband looked happy and fit—far from the man who was always 'too tired' to take me out on the boat or come with me to the health club. I wondered if Ted had a portrait of the couch potato he'd once been, hidden in the attic. Sort of a pudgy Dorian Gray.

But back to Caron, who was obviously far wilier than me, despite her freckled face and button nose. She knew that the competition was a veritable smorgasbord of *baristi,* with the best in the business there for the picking.

And we did need a barista. Enough of the long days and lonely nights. And, bless her, not only did Caron know where to find a barista, she had set her sights high.

Amy was legendary. She was more rock star than barista. She had piercings. Lots of them. And racing-striped hair. And tattoos.

Truth is, I admire people who march to a different drummer—or, in Amy's case, dance to an alternative rock band. I was just stunned that Caron wanted that band playing in our store.

'Wait a second,' I said. 'Remember when we used to hang out at Janalee's Place?' That would be back when we *drank* lattes instead of making them. In other words, the good old days. 'You told me you thought Amy looked like the Antichrist.'

Caron just grinned. 'Amy rocks, Maggy.'

There's something pathetic about a forty-something talking like an eighteen-year-old.

'Listen, I like her, too,' I said. 'But Amy manages Janalee's Place. For your friend, Marvin LaRoche.'

But Caron's face was glowing with an unnatural light. 'Amy's the best, Maggy.' She put her hand over her heart. 'You must get her for me.'

Too weird, but I was starting to understand, at least. Amy was a status symbol for Caron. Like driving a Mercedes or carrying the right handbag. 'You want a designer barista,' I said, flatly. 'What is she? Gucci? Fendi? Prada?'

'Nah,' Sarah piped in. 'Amy's edgier. Maybe Marc Jacobs.'

I shot Sarah a disbelieving look. I wasn't sure which was more amazing—that Caron wanted a trophy barista, or that Sarah knew what a designer was.

Caron reached over and took my hand. 'Marvin La-Roche doesn't deserve her.'

On that, at least, we could agree.

'It's not going to be easy,' Caron continued, as I tried to take back my hand. 'Amy has worked for Janalee since she was in high school. But I do hear there's some friction between Amy and Marvin. You can work that angle.'

'Why am *I* working any angle?' I asked. 'Like I said, if you think this is such a good idea, you run the competition. Or if all we want is a barista, why don't you just call Amy and make her an offer?'

Caron and Sarah exchanged looks.

Sarah finally answered. 'We already have. She refused.'

'We wanted to get her for you for your birthday,' Caron added. 'So you could have sex.'

'For the record, I'm heterosexual.' At least so far. My forty-third birthday had been just last week.

'Don't be an idiot,' Sarah snapped. 'We want you to have sex with that sheriff of yours, Pavlik.'

A noble goal. And one that a barista, who could take the occasional early shift, would admittedly facilitate.

'Besides,' Caron said, 'I think you could use some time away from the store. You're a little…intense these days.'

Intense? I was *intense?*

'You've assigned seats.' Sarah pointed to the wall where I'd tacked up a notice that read: This seat reserved for Henry. If you're NOT Henry, keep your butt off.

Henry Wested lived at the senior center across the street from Uncommon Grounds. He had come in once a day since we'd opened, like clockwork. Lately though, he had taken to visiting a second time, forgetting he'd already been there. Or he didn't come in at all. It worried me.

'Henry gets confused if there's anybody sitting in his chair,' I said, a slightly defensive tone creeping into my voice.

'And you made Jodi McCarthy and Mary Smith sit together last week,' Caron said, 'and you know their sons are competing for starting quarterback at Brookhills High. Jodi and Mary hate each other.'

I snorted. 'Then they should grow up. Besides, the tennis moms needed a table, and there were four of them. I didn't want them to walk out.'

'Like Mrs Doherty did, when she said you were using the froth on her latte to make dirty pictures?'

'That was Princess Leia,' I said, through clenched teeth. 'From *Star Wars*.'

'Looked like a schlong to me,' Sarah muttered, as Caron pushed the button to brew another shot of espresso.

This time it took twenty-three seconds to pass through the grounds. Caron had timed it perfectly. I reached over, took the shot from her and tipped it into the mug.

Sarah waggled her head. 'Besides, just *think* of all the people you'll get to push around at Java Ho.'

'Don't you have somewhere else to be?' I asked her, adding the milk.

'In fact, I do,' she said. 'I need to see Janalee at three thirty. Come with me and talk to Marvin.'

I started to say no, but figured, what the hell? Why let LaRoche and HotWired hog the spotlight? Managing the barista competition would not only increase Uncommon Grounds' visibility in the industry, it would also let me keep tabs on LaRoche. Maybe make his life a living hell for the weekend.

Suddenly, this was sounding better and better.

Besides, Caron was right: I *did* need a change of scenery, and this way I could enjoy the entire barista competition without feeling like I was ducking out on her. In fact, my partner was encouraging me to play hooky.

Sold. I ruined the picture-perfect latte by slopping it into a to-go cup. 'You win,' I said, handing the cup to Sarah. 'Let's go, so I can be "intense" with LaRoche.'

'Don't forget about Amy,' Caron called after us.

MARVIN LAROCHE'S OFFICE was above his newest store, which meant it would take us all of two minutes to reach it.

'You know, a little exercise wouldn't hurt you,' I said, as Sarah revved up her 1975 lemon-yellow Firebird. 'We *could* walk.'

She slapped the transmission into reverse. 'It's nearly a mile, Maggy. That's not exercise, it's insanity.'

'It's six-tenths of a mile,' I said. 'I measured.'

'You would,' Sarah muttered as we pulled out of the parking lot and on to Civic Drive. At the corner, she turned right onto Brookhill Road.

I'd researched traffic patterns and we'd ultimately decided to locate Uncommon Grounds in Benson Plaza, a glorified strip mall on the southeast corner of Civic and Brookhill Road. Brookhill was the main drag into the city and I knew we'd attract commuters who wanted to pick up coffee for their drive to work.

Unfortunately, HotWired's newest location offered that same convenience, and LaRoche hadn't needed to do any research to find that out. Not only had *I* done it, but I'd been stupid enough to tell him about it.

I had met LaRoche at last year's Java Ho and had considered him the pinnacle of my conference networking. What a find! Marvin LaRoche seemed to know everyone in coffee. He had been our coffee fairy godfather, acting as a sounding board and advising us as we were learning the ropes. After all, LaRoche said, that's what people in the industry do for newcomers, assuming they weren't in their market area.

Well, now we were in his market—or more precisely, he was in ours. And I didn't like it a bit.

We passed Schultz's Market and my stomach, always open to suggestion, growled. The store was a little pricey, but they had great produce, seafood and wine. Even better, they also prepared what I called TiVo-dinners. Fresh precooked meals you could take home, heat up and enjoy in front of your favorite digitally recorded movies and shows.

Tonight, though, I planned to cook. Given my schedule and lack of funds, I was trying to eat healthier these days. And cheaper. While TiVo-dinners were good, they sure weren't cheap.

Maybe a nice piece of tilapia. If I blackened it…

A red Probe suddenly darted out of Schultz's parking lot, cutting us off. Sarah slammed on her brakes. The old Firebird didn't have shoulder harnesses, but since I routinely keep one hand braced on the dashboard when I ride with Sarah, I was able to save my face.

'Damn it, McNamara,' Sarah screamed. 'I have a sixteen-year-old kid who's a better driver!'

The car windows being closed, this was lost on Kate McNamara, editor of *The Brookhills Observer*. Nearly deafened me, though.

'She's going to HotWired,' I said, rubbing my left ear. 'You just watch.'

Sarah glanced over at me. 'Been losing customers to them?'

I shrugged. 'Haven't noticed.'

'*You* haven't noticed?' She turned into the HotWired parking lot. 'That's hard to believe.'

I sighed. 'To be honest, I'm trying *not* to notice. Caron says I'm driving people crazy. Sophie Daystrom didn't come in for a week and I nearly gave her a stroke, questioning her about where she was. Turns out the poor old thing had been visiting her daughter in Florida.' Sophie was one of the seniors who frequented Uncommon Grounds.

I undid the seatbelt and started to climb out of the car.

'Sophie has two sons,' Sarah said.

That stopped me. 'No daughters?'

Sarah shook her head. 'Nope.'

Great, not only were the seniors defecting, I'd managed to frighten an eighty-one-year-old woman into lying to me. Mom would be so proud.

I got out, slammed the car door and tried not to look at the other cars in the HotWired parking lot.

'A Lexus, an Infiniti, two Hyundais and a Jaguar,' Sarah reported as she got out the other side. 'Extra points for the Jaguar, right?'

'Double,' I agreed automatically. Then I caught myself. 'But I'm not keeping track.'

I have a nasty habit of counting vehicles in competitors' parking lots to see how we compare. Sometimes I even factor in make and model (two Hyundais equals one Saab, or half a Jaguar convertible).

Sarah rolled her eyes. 'You can't help yourself, Maggy. It's who you are.'

She had a point, which was one of the reasons I'd avoided the new HotWired until now. I figured if I started counting cars or scouting for our regulars, I'd end up bouncing back and forth between Uncommon Grounds and HotWired like some overly competitive, mathematically deranged ping-pong ball.

'Kate's Probe isn't here?' I asked. That was a relief, at least. Kate McNamara could be a pain in the butt, but she was a steady customer.

'She hid it behind the building.'

'Oh.'

I have to admit: I was hurt. First Sophie, now Kate. It was like when I found out Ted was cheating on me, but this time I'd been tossed aside for a bad cup of coffee. I took a deep breath. As Bonnie Raitt says, you can't make someone love you. *Or* your coffee.

'This HotWired is a carbon copy of the others,' I said, trying to change the subject. 'You'd think Janalee would push for a little originality.'

As I mentioned, Janalee had owned the first store of what was to become the HotWired chain long before she ever met LaRoche. Janalee's Place was located in a big old house on the northern, less chi-chi side of town. That would be *my* side of town. The comfortably shabby original might be the genesis of HotWired, but it certainly wasn't the prototype. In my opinion, it had twice the personality of the high-tech, *Matrix*-meets-mocha feel of the newer HotWired stores.

Sarah locked the Firebird. 'I said "carbon copy" the other day to Sam, and he said I was dating myself, that nobody uses carbon paper anymore. "Clone" apparently is the in-word.'

'I think the word "in-word" is out,' I said. 'Besides, isn't a clone, literally, a "carbon" copy?'

As we made for the door, Sarah ignored my scientific input. 'Besides, if Janalee was going to push LaRoche to do anything, it would be all that natural crap.'

All that 'natural crap', as Sarah put it, was Fair Trade and shade-grown coffees, along with dairy products that were free of growth hormones. Fair Trade coffees were beans that were certified grown in a way that was environmentally friendly and also provided fair wages for the people who grew and harvested them. Shade-grown coffees preserved forests that would otherwise be clear-cut to plant coffee.

From its inception, Janalee's Place had been 'a coffeehouse with a social conscience' and Amy carried on that tradition. Social conscience, though, didn't come without a price, and even if Marvin LaRoche hadn't tinkered with Janalee's Place, he'd put his own 'green' stamp—the one with dollar signs—on the new stores.

At Uncommon Grounds, there was always an undertone of conversation, punctuated by greetings for new arrivals. When we walked into HotWired, the undertone was the click-clack of computer keys, and the enthusiastic 'Welcome!' was followed by 'You've got mail!'

I thought I heard a familiar voice in all the cyber hustle and bustle and turned just in time to see Sophie Daystrom duck behind a computer screen. I saw something else, too. A gray fedora lay on the stool that had been pulled out beside the computer.

'That's Henry's hat,' I whispered to Sarah. 'The traitor. How could he do that to me? I reserved his chair. Put up a sign and everything.'

Sarah grabbed my arm and tried to propel me away. 'Rise above it, Maggy. Don't let them know they've hurt you.'

'Hurt, shmurt. That sign's going *down*. Henry's going—'

'Look, Maggy, there's Janalee.' Sarah sounded like she was placating a crabby two-year-old. Which was probably about the right level of maturity for the way I was acting.

I turned reluctantly.

In the midst of all the high-tech activity, Janalee La-Roche was an island of calm. A tall, blue-eyed blonde, Janalee favored peasant skirts, vests in natural fabrics and espadrilles—those canvas sandals with the woven platform soles. I would have looked like Heidi in the get-up, but Janalee managed 'chic' even with a baby hammocked across her chest.

'Is that a coffee bag?' I asked.

The baby was in a sling-type carrier, seemingly fashioned from one of the burlap bags used to ship coffee beans.

Janalee came toward us with a smile. 'Maggy, Sarah. How good to see you. And yes, it is a coffee bag, Maggy. One of the 154-pound bags from Colombia. Little Davy just loves it.' She patted the baby's red cheek. 'Don't you, sweetie?'

'Little Davy' looked like he wanted to be anywhere but in the bag. He let out a yowl.

'I think he's leaking.' Sarah pointed toward a growing wet patch on the carrier.

Janalee reached around and felt it. 'I'm afraid it's one of the perils of using cloth diapers,' she said. 'But nothing but the best for my little boy and the world he lives in. Isn't that right, Davy?'

She was talking in that annoying sing-song baby voice, the one I no doubt had used when Eric was little. Being a new mother is a little like getting drunk in public. It's only in hindsight that you realize what a fool you made of yourself.

'Don't you use rubbers?' Sarah asked.

'Maybe Davy was unplanned,' Janalee said, drawing herself up indignantly, 'but—'

'No, no.' I elbowed Sarah in the ribs. 'I think Sarah meant rubber *pants.*'

'Ohhhhh.' The smile came back. 'Actually, Sarah, I use organic wool diaper covers, instead of rubber or plastic pants. The wool is not only more environmentally friendly, but it holds thirty percent of its weight in urine without feeling damp. The wool cover doesn't lock in the wetness next to Davy's little bum, like rubber pants would. When I'm at home, I let him go with just the cloth diaper. So freeing, don't you think?'

Frankly, Sarah looked like she didn't give a damn about freeing little Davy's butt.

I jumped in. 'Don't disposables wick the moisture away?' I asked in a mother-to-mother tone.

Janalee's hand went to her mouth. 'Six *thousand* disposable diapers go into landfills for each baby. Can you believe that, Maggy?'

Well, Eric and I had certainly done our part. Somewhere there was probably a landfill named for us.

'That is just a great baby carrier,' I gushed, trying to steer the subject away from me and waste management. 'Did you get it at Evram's?'

Janalee gasped. 'No, no—this is from Rene at Coffee Roasters of Las Vegas. You don't buy anything at Evram's department store, do you, Maggy? They use child labor from Third World countries.'

Way to go, Maggy. Right back in the toilet.

I turned toward the office, leaving Sarah to talk to Janalee.

It pained me to admit it, but Marvin LaRoche might well be a saint.

FOUR

LIKE I SAID, I'D NEVER been to this particular HotWired, but since LaRoche valued the cookie-cutter approach to business, I knew where to find him: the loft.

HotWired shops were two stories high—airy and open to the roofline in the front, with a loft/office forming a partial second floor in the rear of the building. Large windows in the office overlooked the coffeehouse floor. It was a great layout for keeping an eye on your employees or picking off the enemy as she climbs the metal steps to breach your position.

I have a fear of heights. Did I mention that?

It's not so much that I'm scared I'm going to fall, as I think I might just go crazy and toss myself over. Freud, Jung, Skinner: have a go at me. Bring your friends. If you have any.

Anyway, clanging my way up the iron-pipe stairway held together by assorted nuts, bolts and, I hoped, heavy-duty lock washers, made me nervous. As I climbed, I asked myself what I was doing there. Not only was LaRoche a worm, he made me feel stupid. And I hated to feel stupid. So why put myself through it? Maybe I should just leave.

Too late. The door above me opened abruptly and LaRoche stared down at me. Sort of. With a shock, I realized the man was slightly cross-eyed. How could I have missed that?

I'd always thought LaRoche was a little shifty-looking, even when he was being 'faux friendly' to us. Had I just been reacting to the fact he was cross-eyed? Maybe it made me vaguely uneasy, even if I hadn't quite registered why.

Geez, if that was true, I was dirt. Insensitive, prejudiced dirt. I held out my hand to him.

LaRoche took it and turned it over to plant a kiss on the palm. 'Coming to negotiate terms of surrender, Maggy?' He grinned and turned away, leaving the door open for me to follow.

OK, *he* was dirt. Cross-eyed dirt. Smiling, cross-eyed dirt. I wiped off my hand on my pants.

'Surrender?' I asked, following him in. 'Whatever do you mean, Marvin?' I could be charming, too. Faux charming.

'Do I smell a story here?' a female voice asked. Kate McNamara, aforementioned editor and crappy driver, stood by LaRoche's desk, sorting through papers in her briefcase.

More likely what she smelled was over-roasted coffee beans, but Kate probably wouldn't know the difference anyway.

LaRoche shook his head. 'I was merely teasing Maggy, Kate. I've been re-reading Sun Tzu's *The Art of War.*' He nodded to a slim book on his desk. 'I'm afraid I have military maneuvers on my mind.'

And all over his office. On the shelves next to LaRoche's desk, miniature toy soldiers did battle on three levels, the books behind them forming a backdrop. One tiny soldier was even tied to a string, apparently rappelling to the shelf below to land on a tome about the Battle of Normandy.

'Guess he's going up, not down,' I murmured.

LaRoche seemed startled, then he saw what I was looking at. He tipped his head in approval. 'Quite right. Scaling the cliffs of Normandy.'

The way he said it made me think of a professor who had just been surprised by a student he believed was a dolt. Little did he know I'd just watched *The Longest Day* on DVD the prior week.

Kate looked like a dolt herself for a second, but recovered nicely and handed LaRoche a paper. I figured she'd be Googling 'cliffs + Normandy + toy soldier' within five minutes of getting to her office. 'Here's your copy of the ad contract, Marvin.'

Kate turned to me. 'You should be advertising, too, Maggy. Offering free drink coupons, like HotWired. People would love it.'

My first thought was that if we spent money on ads, it wouldn't be in a glorified shopper like *The Brookhills Observer*. My second thought was, Free drink coupons?

LaRoche was nodding. 'It's a great way to get people in the door.'

Also a great way to bankrupt your competition. Free drinks for a week was one thing, but if HotWired gave them away for any length of time…

'So, Marvin,' Kate said, picking up her briefcase and crossing to the door, 'we'll just automatically renew in thirty days. You tell us when to stop.' She smiled, all teeth and glossy black hair and freckles. I wanted to stomp her.

This was my worst nightmare.

Well, this and not being able to get to the basement before a tornado comes. My 'I'm hurrying, but not getting anywhere' dream. Now that Ted and I were divorced, the nightmare had devolved into an 'I'm trying to get to the basement, but there *is* no basement' dream.

Scary enough, but a competitor with pockets sufficiently deep to give away their product until they ran you out of business? That was right up there with tornadoes—with or without basements—believe me.

Sarah's 'Don't let them know they've hurt you' reverberated in my head. 'Don't shoot until you see the whites of their eyes' was bouncing around in there, too, for some reason.

I smiled back at Kate. 'I'll think about that advertising. Thanks.' In fact, I had a feeling I'd have trouble *not* thinking about the advertising. Especially around three a.m.

LaRoche said goodbye to Kate and closed the door behind her. He didn't seem at all upset she had blabbed about the ads. Probably hoped I'd be intimidated.

He picked up *The Art of War.* 'As I was saying, Maggy. If you're a student of military gamesmanship, you really must read this.'

'I'm afraid I don't think killing, or being killed, is much of a game,' I said dryly.

'Such a female way of looking at it.' He laughed, his blue eyes and white teeth flashing in contrast to his Fake n' Bake tan. 'It's all about strategy, Maggy. Tactics.

And that's a game we play every day in business—' a yowl from Little Davy downstairs— 'or in our personal lives.'

I eyed Sun Tzu's book, which I actually *had* read at the suggestion of a colleague twenty years ago. Two decades, but that was just a drop in the bucket for the Chinese general's book. Sun Tzu had been born around 500 BC. Which just went to show you, nothing really changes. Especially human nature.

Flip-flop BOING, flip-flop BOING, flip-flop BOING. Janalee was coming up the stairs in her thick-soled espadrilles. I hoped the *BOING* wasn't Davy's head hitting the metal railing as the baby-sling swung with every step. Encouragingly, I didn't hear crying, though I guess that could have meant either unscathed or unconscious.

Janalee tapped on the door and came in. Davy's bulky carrier was under one arm. In the opposite hand, Janalee carried a big brown paper bag. The woman was a packhorse. How in the world had she scaled the steep steps like that?

Janalee divested herself of the brown bag—presumably the *boing* of the *flip-flop BOING*—and fished Davy out of the sling. She set him down on the pine-planked floor.

'Janalee, dear,' LaRoche said, eying Davy as the baby settled himself next to his father's battle-shelves. 'Can I help you with something?'

While the words said one thing, the tone said something altogether different. Something not very nice.

But Janalee just smiled. 'Sarah told me that Maggy has volunteered to oversee the barista competition, and I wanted to thank her and turn over the files.'

I guessed that explained what Sarah needed to see Janalee about.

'Really?' LaRoche turned to me. 'That's a marvelous idea, Maggy. It's a very visible position, and Uncommon Grounds could certainly use the exposure.'

I hate this man, I hate this man, I hate this man.

I gritted my teeth and smiled—it's harder than it sounds. 'I would *love* to take over the competition.' Especially if that competition was HotWired.

I was looking at Marvin when I said it, but Janalee answered. 'Thank you so much, Maggy. You're a lifesaver.'

She pulled a big stack of files out of the bottom of the baby sling. I wondered if she had a Volkswagen and clowns in there, too.

'It was no problem doing the upfront arrangements,' Janalee was saying, 'but with Davy...' She gestured to where the baby was now standing, having pulled himself up on the bookshelves to grab the dangling soldier. He'd left a puddle on the floor—apparently the 'organic wool diaper cover' had reached its thirty-percent organic-wool saturation point. '...starting to get around, it would be impossible for me to get anything done.' She handed me the files.

They felt a little damp, so I took them gingerly. 'Thanks, Janalee. I'll call you if I have any questions after looking them over.'

Which would be subsequent to drying and disinfecting them.

LaRoche nodded in approval. 'I'm sure you'll do a bang-up job, Maggy. I'm head judge, so don't hesitate to turn to me for advice.'

Right. That had worked out so well once before. 'Thank you, Marvin, but I was an event manager in my PR life, remember? I think I'll be able to handle it.'

In truth, I hadn't the faintest idea what to do. I'd only seen *one* barista competition in my life. Not that I was going to tell LaRoche that. As his hero, Sun Tzu, had said, 'The opportunity of defeating the enemy is provided by the enemy himself.' I didn't intend to provide LaRoche with anything, especially information on my possible shortcomings.

But LaRoche wasn't paying any attention to me. He was staring at the coffeehouse floor below us, where ground zero of the Battle for the Barista had just walked in.

Amy.

She was with a gray-haired man, who towered over the five-foot-two-inch, rainbow-haired, multiply-pierced barista by a full foot. I recognized the man as Levitt Fredericks, president of EarthBean, a consortium of store owners and roasters who worked for environmentally friendly trade practices.

'Now what's *he* doing here?' It was like LaRoche had given voice to my thoughts. Except in my head, the question was followed by, Has LaRoche grown a conscience?

Not that I had any right to talk, really. While Caron and I stocked Fair Trade and shade-grown coffees, we didn't carry them exclusively, much to Levitt Fredericks' dismay.

'Amy and Levitt are friends, Marvin,' Janalee said. 'You know that.'

Amy had worked for Janalee long before LaRoche had appeared on the scene, making her the obvious choice to take over the store when Janalee had gone from making coffee to making...Davy. Word had it that despite her heavy-on-the-metal appearance, Amy was a genuine environmentalist. The rainbow hair and tattoos? Henna, I suspected, though I didn't share that with anyone. Every town needs a legend.

Janalee had turned her attention to preventing the soldier-on-a-rope from dying a watery death in the pool of baby pee. 'Davy,' she said gently, 'let's put Daddy's toy down.'

But patience apparently wasn't one of Daddy's virtues. 'Friends,' he said, mimicking Janalee's saccharine tone. 'Exactly what does *that* mean?'

Tossing the Sun Tzu book on the desk, LaRoche snatched the soldier from Davy. The look the one-year-old gave him in response was pure Damien—the original *Omen* Damien. Even I hadn't wasted any time with the sequels.

I cleared my throat uncomfortably, wanting out.

Janalee gestured toward the brown paper bag on the desk. 'That's the first-place trophy. It's a barista, as interpreted by a local artist. I'm having the rest of the trophies shipped directly to your attention at the convention center.'

I shifted the stack of folders to my left arm in order to pick up the trophy. Most of the files were facedown, but I caught a glimpse of a tab marked 'Competitive Strategies.'

Whose strategies? I wondered. Janalee's? Or, more interestingly, Marvin's?

In an old cartoon, a light bulb would have appeared above my head. I had an idea. A strategy, even.

I'd been maneuvered into taking over the barista competition, right? Now it was up to me to make sure that Uncommon Grounds got as much visibility as possible out of it, especially since we didn't have a barista participating.

Well, what was more visible than television?

I still had connections, after all. I'd talk one of the local stations into covering the event. I could see it now: *Iron Barista,* like *Iron Chef America* on Food Network. Maybe I could even trademark and syndicate it.

A menacing sound from Davy interrupted my thoughts. Father and son were still glaring at each other. Any second now, LaRoche would call the kid out and give him his choice of weapons. If it was wet diapers at twenty paces, my money was on Davy.

I was out of there. As I turned to leave, I saw Sun Tzu's book on the desk. Why just win the Battle for the Barista, when I could win the whole war? Or at least go down fighting.

I grabbed the book and stuck it in with the trophy. 'Thanks for offering to lend me *The Art of War,* Marvin,' I said. 'I would love to reread it.'

LaRoche, still holding the toy soldier, turned. He looked like he'd forgotten I was there, and he certainly had forgotten offering to lend me the book. Since he hadn't.

I tapped my forehead. 'Remind me. Wasn't it Sun Tzu who said something like, "Know thy enemy"?'

LaRoche gave me that 'she's-smarter-than-she-looks' expression again. '"If you know the enemy and know yourself",' he quoted, '"you needn't fear the result of a hundred battles."'

'Sort of keep your friends close and your enemies even closer, huh?'

He set down the soldier. 'Sort of,' he said, mimicking me like he had Janalee.

I just smiled. 'Then I'll look forward to seeing you Thursday.'

With that, I retreated down the steps, armed with six damp file folders, a bubble-wrapped barista, and the words of a 2500-year-old Chinese general.

FIVE

SARAH MET ME AT THE bottom of the stairs. 'Well?'

Before answering, I glanced over to where Henry's hat had been. The fedora was gone. As was the top of Sophie's head. I could just imagine Henry reaching up from behind the counter to retrieve the hat, and then the two seniors scurrying out the back hand in hand, like rats deserting a sinking ship. Not that rats have hands to hold. Or that Sophie and Henry had ever held them, to my knowledge. Besides, it wasn't HotWired that was in danger of sinking. It was Uncommon Grounds.

So much for similes. Or metaphors. Or whatever the hell they were. I turned back to Sarah. 'Well, *what?*' I demanded.

'So are you going to do it? Are you going to manage the barista competition?'

Sarah sounded enthusiastic. Sarah *never* sounded enthusiastic. Cynical, sure. And she had a corner on the market of snide, but enthusiastic? Nah. Maybe she was putting on a show for the man up above.

I glanced at LaRoche in his loft and, sure enough, he was watching us.

'Not only am I going to manage the barista competition, Sarah,' I said, beaming a big cheesy smile up at LaRoche before turning back, 'I'm going to make it a star.'

Sarah's eyes narrowed. 'You still watching those old movies? You're starting to talk like one.'

I linked arms with her and started walking her toward the door. 'The moon, Sarah. We can have the stars *and* the moon.'

'*Now Voyager,* 1942,' she snapped, pulling away. Not a toucher, our Sarah—apparently not even to impress her biggest client. 'And Bette Davis' line is, "Don't let's ask for the moon. We have the stars." If you're going to quote movies, Maggy, at least get 'em right.'

Now *there* was the Sarah I knew and loved, though sometimes I wasn't sure why. I liked to think I was neither insecure nor a masochist, just perceptive enough to see the genuinely good person buried under all of Sarah's bluster. Some days it might take a backhoe to reach it, but then I was no picnic, either.

Safely out the door, I reverted to character, too. 'We're doomed, Sarah.' I moaned. 'Doomed, do you hear me?'

'Stop the theatrics, Maggy!' Sarah snarled. 'Do you hear *me?*'

She was right. I couldn't afford to panic now. Not about HotWired and their free drinks coupons, or about the possible annihilation of life as I knew it.

I had a plan. A strategy, as LaRoche would put it. First step was:

1. Call Mark.

That was pretty much my plan, so far. My friend Mark headed up one of the local TV stations and, as soon as we got back to Uncommon Grounds, I would put a call into him and ask his advice.

As we climbed into the Firebird, I filled Sarah in on HotWired's impending barrage of free-drink coupons and my idea for the televised competition.

'It's Tuesday, and the competition starts Friday,' she pointed out as she turned the ignition key. 'Isn't three days pushing it to get the Chairman and the gang from *Iron Chef America* to Brookhills? Long as you're dreaming, maybe Martin Scorsese could drop by and direct.'

Leave it to Sarah to put her finger on the crux of the matter. And then bury it up to the knuckle.

'Very funny.' The g-force of the Firebird's acceleration pinned me to the seat. I wondered if my cheeks were flapping in the wind like a bloodhound's with its head stuck out the window of a pickup truck. 'I'm not stupid. I know that whatever we can put together this year will be barebones—more of a test run than anything else— but it would give us a tape to show people toward next year.'

'Show who people?'

While the syntax needed work, I knew what Sarah meant. Problem was I didn't have the answer to her question. Did you pitch a network with an idea like this? Or a production company? Or maybe public TV? I didn't know. Hence my call to Mark.

'I'm not sure,' I admitted, 'but I know people who know, which is more than half the battle. I'm thinking we may even be able to syndicate. Go national.'

Apparently I'd finally managed to capture Sarah's imagination. 'You need a catchy name.' She glanced over at me. 'Whatcha going to call it, *Iron Barista?*'

'Only if I wanted a lawsuit,' I said.

'There's no such thing as bad publicity.'

'Yeah, so say people who have the money to ride out the bad publicity,' I said. 'No, it would have to be something unrelated to anything that's on the air. I'm figuring it would essentially be the semis and the finals of the competition as it's staged now, with the six finalists preparing three different drinks.'

'KiloCup, MegaCup and GigaCup?' Sarah made the quick left onto Civic and another hard left into our parking lot, tires squealing.

Kilo, Mega, Giga. HotWired's 'byte-sized' drinks. I righted myself and rolled my eyes. 'Again, very funny. Nicotine deprivation becomes you.'

A withering glance from Sarah.

I got out of the car. 'The three drinks *I'm* talking about are an espresso, a cappuccino and a signature drink—one that's theirs and theirs alone. The contestants make four of every kind, one for each of the sensory judges, who judge them on everything from the color of the espresso, to the consistency of the foam, to the china used to present the drink.'

'Sounds fascinating, but we're talking television here,' Sarah said, still sitting in the driver's seat. 'Do people get hysterical when they're eliminated? Maybe throw cups?'

I had closed my door, so I was forced to walk around to the other side of the car to continue the conversation. I thought as I walked. Sarah had a point.

'Maybe some backbiting,' I admitted when I got there. 'But it normally wouldn't escalate into violence. On the other hand, there is a lot of stress, not to mention hot water, steam, breakable objects. With the proper editing—'

'Back to the name,' Sarah interrupted. 'You know what you should call this?'

'Maybe *Uncommon Barista?*' I ventured. 'Then the show would have a natural tie-in to Uncommon Grounds.'

Which was the one problem with my idea, of course. How did I maintain control of something—the barista competition—of which I had no ownership? The telecast was my idea, of course, but could you copyright…?

'No, no, no.' Sarah was shaking her head. 'You, with all your movies, I can't believe you didn't think of this.'

'Of *what?*' I was getting impatient. I wanted to go in and call Mark. Maybe move on to Step Two or Three, whatever they might be.

But Sarah wasn't ready to give yet. 'So when people are eliminated they have to leave, right? Some host, maybe you, gives them the boot?'

Maybe me. It wasn't a bad idea. I'd done TV before, after all. It was a few years back, but…

'*Right?*' Apparently I hadn't answered fast enough for Sarah.

'Right,' I agreed. 'Soooo?'

'Soooo—' Sarah revved the motor of the Firebird— 'when they lose it's… "Hasta Barista, Baby!"'

And with a wave of her hand and the screech of her tires, Sarah was gone, leaving me in a haze of burning rubber.

It was only when I stepped into the store that I realized I'd forgotten to talk to Amy.

SIX

'WELL? DID YOU TALK TO AMY?' Caron demanded, wiping her hands on her apron.

She'd just finished cleaning the espresso machine, despite the fact we didn't close for another half hour.

Ignoring her, I pulled out my cellphone and punched in Mark's number. Funny how I could remember a phone number I hadn't dialed for a year, but still couldn't...

'What did you say? What did she say?' Caron was asking eagerly.

I held up my hand as the outgoing voice mail message on the other end of the phone ended. 'Hey, Mark,' I said after the beep. Then I realized the voice on the recording had been neither Mark nor his secretary, Jamie. I didn't have time to leave a message on an old number.

'Never mind,' I said into the phone. I pressed 'O' in hopes of connecting with a human being. It worked.

'Hello,' I said to aforementioned human being. 'Could you connect me with Mark Strachota?'

'Your name, please?' the woman asked.

I told her.

'Could you spell that?'

I did.

'And how may I help you?'

I told her.

'Mark who?' she asked.

'Mark Strachota.' I was trying to be patient. After all, I could be talking to a computer chip.

'Could you spell that?'

'S…t…r…' I continued with each letter, rolling my eyes at Caron.

'Did you dial the right number?' Caron asked in a stage whisper.

I nodded.

'And you pronounce that, how?' the woman was asking.

'Station manager,' I said flatly. OK, so I was losing it.

'Could you hold?' she asked. I was listening to canned music before I could respond.

'They're transferring me,' I said to Caron hopefully. I'm a cup-half-full kind of person. 'Now what were you saying?'

'So what did you tell Amy?' Caron asked eagerly. 'Did you tell her we'll top her salary at HotWired? Promise her we'll go all-green?'

'What? You didn't want me to offer her my first-born?' Barry Manilow was singing 'Copacabana' in my ear.

'Eric and Amy are about the same age,' Caron said, now attacking the smoothie machine. 'Just think: grandchildren with Eric's brains and Amy's piercings.'

'I thought you were a fan of Amy's piercings.'

'Copacabana' morphed into a dial tone. I flipped the phone closed. 'And stop cleaning that damn machine,' I said irritably, 'or we'll have the entire seventh grade of Brookhills Middle School in here ordering smoothies at two minutes to six.'

'Cleaning the machines doesn't bring in customers any more than washing your car makes it rain.' She looked up from where she was swishing the blender container in hot soapy water. 'And *have* you washed that filthy van of yours lately?'

I shrugged. 'Why tempt the rain gods?' My old Dodge Caravan—remnant of my past life—wouldn't be much improved by a carwash anyway. A car-*crusher,* maybe.

'So by your way of thinking, if you keep this up we're in for a drought.'

'Drought?' a voice said. 'Oh, is *that* what you call it when your customers *desert* you?'

Ahh, Kate McNamara. Turner of the pithy, yet non-sensical, phrase.

Caron—a former copywriter—rolled her eyes and ducked into the office, leaving me to deal with the news-woman. 'Can I get you something, Kate, or are you just here to torture the English language?'

Kate gave me a withering look. 'I thought I'd bring you a rate sheet. You might be wise to consider some advertising of your own.'

When I didn't reach to take the paper she was bran-dishing, she added, 'You know, *I'm* not the enemy here.'

She might have a point. But more importantly, she had a use.

'Listen,' I said. 'I was just trying to call Mark Stra-chota over at TVR.'

Kate had worked at the station as a producer before she decided that it was ink that ran through her veins, not sound bites. Or maybe they just dumped the witch.

'Mark? He took over their sister station in San Diego almost a year ago. It was a fabulous move for him— wherever have you been?'

Up to my ears in coffee beans, obviously. 'Who's taken over? Anyone I'd know?'

'I haven't had the pleasure of meeting him yet, but I hear he's a very bright guy out of Syracuse.' Kate said. She was sucking up to the guy, even in absentia. 'Why?'

Syracuse wouldn't help me. 'Nothing, really. I—'

'You want to televise the barista competition,' she said slowly. 'I heard you're running it.'

Sounded like everyone had known about it except me. I held up my hands. 'Hey, I never said—'

'You didn't have to.' Kate was already digging through her purse for a pen. 'I know how you PR types think. Mark Strachota couldn't have done anything for you anyway, except perhaps get you some news coverage. Network affiliates can't turn on a dime like that. Now, *cable,* though...' She'd found the pen and was tapping it rapid-fire on the rate sheet.

I took the pen away from her. 'I thought about cable, of course—Food Network, Discovery, Travel Channel. But wouldn't they need even *more* time?'

'Not my station.' She grinned at me, and even her Irish eyes were smiling. 'Bet you didn't know I'm also doing on-air now.'

On-air? Kate McNamara was not going to be the on-air talent for my show, not as long as I...

'Wait a second. Are you talking about the local cable access station? What do you do there? The school lunch menu?'

Kate looked hurt. 'For all three schools. Kindergarten through grade twelve. And I do school closings during the winter.'

'Tempting as it might be to tap into your audience, Kate, I had something bigger in mind. Maybe—'

'Listen to me, Maggy.' She got in my face. 'You need me. You are *three* days away from the competition. The best you can hope for now is a demo tape you can show to all those networks you're fantasizing about, in hopes of putting together something for next year.'

Local cable access. A tad deflating, but Kate was just reinforcing what I'd said to Sarah earlier. I'd hoped, though, for a little more than a kid with a camcorder. 'How—'

Kate's conversation mirrored her interview technique: she never let the subject get a word in edgewise. 'I have access to an editing suite, cameras, operators, editors.'

'High school students?' I asked doubtfully.

'Don't be silly. College. Brookhills Community College actually runs the station. These young people know more about technology by osmosis than we'll ever be able to learn.'

True. I swear Eric emerged from my womb, text-messaging: 'Brace urself mom im comin out:)'

'So what do you think?' Kate pressed.

What did I think? I thought I was selling my soul to the she-devil. But fact was, it was pretty much a buyers' market these days.

'On one condition,' I said, holding up a finger. 'If this actually makes money at some point, we split seventy–thirty. I'm the seventy. Oh, and I'm also the on-air talent.'

Kate hadn't flinched at the seventy-thirty, but her eyes narrowed at the last. 'You? What kind of experience do you have?'

'I *was* the voice of First National.'

Kate snorted. 'The bank's video newsletter? Please.'

'It sure as hell trumps "chop suey on steamed rice and a carton of fresh Wisconsin milk."'

'Which just illustrates how little you know,' Kate said, sounding petulant. 'The milk comes in bags these days.'

I didn't even want to think about that particular sacrilege. 'I also was interviewed on-camera tons of times.'

'Being interviewed and interviewing someone are two different things.'

A lightbulb went on. I knew Kate wouldn't back down without getting something in return. Maybe this was a bone I could afford to throw her.

'True,' I said and then paused like I was mulling over what she'd said. 'How about this? You're in control of the technical aspects and direction, and I'm in charge of the event itself. You're the reporter, I'm the event spokesman.'

'Just like old times,' Kate said, a flicker in her eyes.

That flicker ignited a memory. Geez, how could I have forgotten? Kate *had* interviewed me once, filling in for an ill reporter. A severe thunderstorm had descended on a fireworks show I was managing. I'd had to cancel the show and send a quarter of a million sodden spectators running for cover.

No one had been hurt, but Kate—who apparently saw this as her ticket to stardom—had seized the opportunity,

trying to get me to admit I'd done something wrong. Ne-
glected to throw a virgin into a volcano or something.
I was having none of it and pointed out, during the live
interview, that I'd been in consultation with her station's
own meteorologist and had acted on his advice.

Kate had turned beet red, stumbling over her 'This
is Katherine McNamara, reporting for TVR TV' in her
haste to sign off.

I figured I'd simply done my job in the face of a
green, overly aggressive reporter. To my knowledge,
Kate had not been 'Katherine McNamara reporting'
anywhere ever again, and I can't say it had bothered me.
In fact, I'd completely forgotten it. But now, as Kate's
smile grew Cheshire cat-size, I wondered if payback
really *was* a bitch.

HAPPILY, THE HORDE of teen smoothie drinkers never
showed up, so Caron and I were able to walk out the door
at the stroke of six. I pulled out my cellphone on the way
to the car and punched a '1'—speed dial for Pavlik. The
sheriff didn't know he was at the top of my contact list,
and I sure wasn't about to tell him.

'Pavlik.'

Short, sweet. Two things Pavlik wasn't.

I cleared my throat. 'This is Maggy.'

'Maggy?'

Had it been so long he didn't remember me? I was
about to give him my last name and spell it, when he
added, 'Your number came up "private" on Caller ID. I
almost didn't answer.'

'I had it blocked,' I said, not bothering to explain why.
Pavlik knew my history.

'So, how are you?' he asked. 'I've been thinking about you.'

'Me, too.'

Pavlik laughed, and I felt myself turn red.

'I meant I was thinking about *you*,' I said hastily.

'Of course,' he said. 'So what have you been thinking about me?' He paused, then softly: 'And, I hope, *us*.'

Oooh, this was going better than I'd dared hope. 'I know this is short notice, but any chance you're free to come over for dinner tonight? Caron opens tomorrow morning, so I can stay up late like a big girl.'

'Me, too. Though in my case, of course, like a big boy.' I could practically hear the dirty grin form on his face.

'Seven thirty?' That would give me time to stop at Schultz's Market, get home, feed Frank, shower and get dinner started.

'Perfect,' he said. 'I'll bring the wine. Red?'

I planned on making fish, but both of us preferred red wine and far be it from me to be a slave to convention. At least to this particular convention. Java Ho might prove to be a whole different thing.

'Yes, please, but probably a lighter one. I'm making fish.'

'Red it is.' And he rang off.

As I pulled into Schultz's Market, I saw Amy's Ford Escape Hybrid parked in the corner of the lot. The reason I noticed the vehicle in the first place was that I was toying with the idea of replacing my old minivan with one. The reason I knew it was Amy's was that she was still sitting in it.

Caron would no doubt want me to take advantage of the opportunity, so I grudgingly maneuvered my van into a nearby spot. Caron and I might be partners, but sometimes I felt like I was working with—or for—my mom.

Which reminded me: I'd forgotten to ask Caron for her recipe for tilapia. She had made it one night when she and Bernie had me over for dinner. Since she said it was easy, I thought I'd cook it for Pavlik tonight. I dug through my purse for the cellphone and punched in Caron's home number. The call went right to voice mail. Damn. I threw the phone back into the abyss, hoping tilapia came with an instruction manual.

But first, Amy.

I turned to look at her silhouette in the Escape. Caron had already approached the barista and been turned down. What did she expect me to do? Win Amy over by the sheer force of my sparkling personality?

Boy, were *we* ever in trouble.

Levering myself out of the van, I slammed the door hard behind me and trudged toward the Escape. I was about ten yards away when I realized Amy was on the phone.

Perfect, I thought. I could acknowledge her and head into the store with a clear conscience and an assuaged partner. I was still about five yards out and ready with my 'don't-want-to-disturb-you' finger-wiggle, when I realized Amy was in tears. Not a little sniffling, but full-bore, snot-flying, cellphone-clogging sobbing.

Veering off, I made for the market door, wondering if Amy's predicament had anything to do with Hot-

Wired. LaRoche certainly had seemed to be nursing a grudge earlier. While I didn't think Janalee would let him fire Amy...

I was so preoccupied with my thoughts that as I entered the 'In' side of the automatic doors at Schultz's, I almost missed Antonio The Milkman coming through the 'Out.' Not wanting to be kicked in the butt by our respective doors, I used my finger-wiggle on him and got a chin salute in return as he continued a phone conversation on his cellphone. Alexander Graham Bell had a lot to answer for.

Once inside the store, I ignored both the red wine on my right and the extra-dark chocolate on my left and made for the seafood counter. Health-food shopping would have to wait.

As bad luck would have it, Jacque Oui, fishmonger to the stars—or what passed for stars in Brookhills—was manning the counter. I almost kept going, but, steeled by thoughts of Pavlik's gratitude at my cooking and the ways he might repay me, I pressed on.

'Hello, Jacque. I need some tilapia.'

When he just stared at me, I added, 'I think. I mean, I thought...maybe...?'

'You *thought.*'

The poor man had given up trying to get me to cook years ago, and since then we had settled into an uneasy truce. I had agreed to smile sheepishly as I passed his counter on the way to the TiVo-dinners and he had agreed to sneer audibly in response.

I cleared my throat. 'No, actually I *know* I need tilapia.'

Jacque eyed me cautiously. Afraid to trust his ears, no doubt.

'I'm going to cook,' I squeaked out.

'You don't know how to cook.'

True. 'So you'll teach me,' I said, trying to channel a little Hepburn hutzpah. Katharine, not Audrey.

'Then you do not want tilapia.' He slid open the glass door of his refrigerated case majestically. 'Today, we will choose halibut.'

'We will?'

'We will. Even *you* will not ruin halibut. How many?' His hand hovered over the fish.

'Umm…'

An eye roll. 'How many people do you have?'

'Two.'

'One would be a female, I take it.' He eyed me and picked out a medium-sized fillet. 'And the other?'

'Male.'

Jacque pulled out a hunk of fish that could have fed the multitudes, providing it was combined with a loaf or two.

'Big enough, you think?' I asked.

'A man needs his strength, no?' Jacque weighed the halibut and then slipped it with the other piece into a plastic bag.

'I sincerely hope so,' I said under my breath.

'Please?' Jacque was spooning shaved ice into a second clear plastic bag.

'Nothing. What are you doing?'

'Putting the fish on ice.' He slipped the plastic bag containing the halibut into the ice-filled bag and then twist-tied that one closed, too, before holding it out to me. 'So that the halibut will stay fresh. Like you.'

Cute. But by this time I was feeling far from fresh. I took the bag gingerly. 'How do I cook it?'

'Simple. Season lightly—salt, pepper, lemon, perhaps—and broil ten to fifteen minutes until the fish flakes with a fork. No more. You understand?'

He was already halfway down the counter, smiling at a woman in tennis togs and matching tennis bracelet. Bet Brookhills Barbie ordered fish more than once a decade.

'Got it. Thanks,' I said, waving at his back.

As I walked toward the checkout, I eyed the plump plastic bag that I was dangling by the twist tie. 'Sort of like bringing home a goldfish,' I muttered.

'Only filleted.'

I looked up and saw Amy in the next line. If I had any doubt that the barista was ecology-conscious, the mascara streaks on her face would have dispelled it. Organic make-up wasn't waterproof. Be-streaked or not, though, Amy had pasted a smile on her face and gone shopping. Me, I head for the clothing store when I want a pick-me-up. Kitchen tools apparently floated Amy's boat.

I grinned at her. 'Maybe if I *had* kept the goldfish on ice, it would have lasted longer than a day.'

'I know,' she said, with a shake of her rainbow-colored hair. 'One day Goldie is in the fishbowl. The next, the toilet bowl.'

'Poor Goldie,' I intoned solemnly. 'Pet store might as well have saved time and sent them home in blue water.'

She laughed and began unloading utensils on to the belt. 'I'm in a rush, but it was good to see you.'

'Same here.' I handed my halibut to the cashier. 'Have a good night.'

The tears resurfaced in Amy's eyes. 'Thanks. I plan to do my best.'

SEVEN

WHEN PAVLIK ARRIVED, I had planned to be showered and dressed, looking totally at ease and casually chic, like I entertained handsome men seven nights a week. I had also planned to have a big ol' glass of wine in my totally at ease, casually chic hand.

Instead, I had a big ol' dog on my chest.

To my mind, Frank is my son's sheepdog—a furry lodger that Eric would reclaim the moment he graduated from college.

In Frank's mind, he is my hairy best friend. Sad thing is, Frank is probably more right than I am.

Sheriff Jake Pavlik stands about six feet tall and has dark curly hair and gray eyes that veer from a brooding black when he is angry to nearly blue when he is amused.

He was amused now. 'I take it you were away too long?'

Flat on my back and buried under 110 pounds of sheepdog and slobber, I didn't bother to protest that I'd been just twenty minutes late. Or that I'd had a dog door installed so Frank could let himself out whenever he needed to.

'Will you get him off me?' I pleaded as Frank tried to lick me on the mouth. I turned my head frantically back and forth to keep him off target. 'Yuck, yuck, yuck... help!!!'

'Puppies lick their mothers' lips as a form of attachment. He's just saying "Hi, Mom."'

'I am not this hairball's mother.' I put up my hands and managed to catch both sides of Frank's collar and push his head up. A string of drool was dangling three inches above my nose. 'And he's two years old, for God's sake. Will you please grab him, dammit?'

'Shame, shame. You kiss your mother with that mouth?' Pavlik was laughing so hard that I thought he was going to fall down. He tugged lightly on Frank's collar and pulled him off. 'Sit, boy.'

Damned if the dog didn't sit. I did, too, brushing myself off. 'How did you do that?'

'Authority.' Pavlik flashed his badge. 'I ooze it.'

'If I wasn't covered in dog slime,' I said, standing up and wiping at my face, 'that might make me hot.'

Pavlik surveyed me. 'If you weren't covered in dog slime, it might make me hot, too.'

Hmm. But maybe this evening could still be salvaged. I leaned down to pick up the Schultz's Market bag from where I'd dropped it when Frank tackled me.

'I think a shower is in order, don't you?' I said lightly. I was half-hoping Pavlik might suggest joining me.

But Frank already had fetched his tennis ball.

'Go get it, Frank, go get it,' Pavlik yelled, pretending to throw the ball and then palming it. It was a game they both loved—the fuzz as much the furball. Hunk of Burning Trust that Frank was, he would race around the yard eagerly looking for the ball before bounding back to Pavlik to be tricked again.

'Great,' Pavlik said, tossing the ball over Frank's head when he wasn't looking. 'Call me when dinner's ready.'

I could only hope that when the tennis ball got as slimy as I was, Pavlik would lose interest in that, too.

THE BROILER WAS PREHEATING and things were warming up between Pavlik and me, too, when his cellphone rang. He picked up.

'Where?' He glanced over at me and then away. I got a little chill. Not the good kind.

'Right, the coffee place—I know it. I'll be right over.' Pavlik flipped the phone closed and slid it into his pocket before he turned to me. 'I have to go.'

'What happened? And at what coffeehouse?'

We were both standing up now and he slipped his arms around me. 'It's a fire, but don't worry. It's not at Uncommon Grounds.'

I nodded, feeling relieved and then feeling ashamed at feeling relieved. Catholic Guilt has nothing on Lutheran Self-loathing. 'Then where?'

'Janalee's Place. And apparently their manager was hurt.' He kissed me and started out the door. I grabbed my jacket and followed.

SINCE PAVLIK HAD his Harley, and I wasn't really dressed for riding a hog, we took separate vehicles. Good thing, because halfway there I realized I hadn't turned off the broiler and had to turn around. By the time I finally arrived at Janalee's Place, the firefighters were winding up hoses and taking off their helmets. Pavlik was deep in conversation with one of his deputies, so I looked around.

Janalee's Place was built of cream city brick, a light yellow brick made during the 1800s from the clay indigenous to the western shore of Lake Michigan. The charming shop had a center door, with a cheerful white-curtained window to each side of it.

Now, though, the facade looked like a pathetic dying creature. The soot from the fire formed ghastly black eyes around the openings where the windows had been, and what was left of the white ruffled curtains flapped listlessly, the only sign of lingering life. The doorway gaped open like a mouth gasping for air.

The sight reminded me of Amy's smudged eyes when I'd seen her at the grocery store. I hunted around and found her sitting just inside the ambulance, her right hand swathed in gauze.

Seeing no one who could tell me not to, I climbed in and sat next to her. 'Amy, are you OK?'

She had been staring off toward the far side of the ambulance—a mere four or five feet, but it could have been a thousand miles away, by the look in her eyes. She jumped.

I put my hand out to steady her. 'I'm so sorry. I didn't mean to startle you.'

'Oh, Maggy. I didn't expect to see anyone, I was just… just…just…' Tears welled up and spilled over, leaving clean streaks down her sooty face.

I pulled a tissue out of my purse and handed it to her. 'You're hurt. Were you alone in the store?'

She nodded. 'This area is mostly commercial so we close at six when the office crowd leaves. I was just dropping off the things I bought at Schultz's.' Her lip quivered. 'I smelled smoke.'

'You didn't go in, did you?' I asked, gesturing toward her bandaged hand.

'I tried.' She shook her head sadly, apparently filled with regret for not having been barbecued. 'But when I grabbed the doorknob...'

'I'm sorry you burned your hand,' I said, ever the mother. 'But that hot doorknob may have saved your life.' I looked back at the remains of the building. 'If you had gone in—'

'Amy? Amy? I came as soon as I heard. Are you hurt?' Janalee—five foot ten and organically grown—climbed into the ambulance, baby on board. It was getting mighty crowded in there.

Amy leapt up. 'I am so sorry, Janalee. I was too late to do anything.'

Janalee took her by the shoulders. 'You have nothing to be sorry about. I'm just glad you're all right.'

A paramedic stuck his head in. 'Hate to break up the party, ladies, but we have to get Ms Caprese to the hospital.'

Ms Caprese? Nice. I hadn't even known Amy's last name, despite the fact that I had known her for three or four years and had been plotting to steal her from Hot-Wired. Yes, and don't think it hadn't crossed my mind that with Janalee's Place gone, Amy might be looking for a job. Good thing I was sensitive enough to let the thought pass right through without trying to entertain it for long.

Speaking of entertaining, I should find out if Pavlik still wanted dinner. I tried to stand up to leave, but with Amy, Janalee and Davy taking up the center of the ambulance, the best I could manage was to slide down the bench and slip sideways out the door.

'Glad you're OK, Amy,' I called back in. 'I'm so sorry about the fire, Janalee.'

The paramedic gave me a sour look as I passed, so I decided to take the low road. 'Could you tell me where to find Sheriff Pavlik?'

He gestured somewhere in the vicinity of Lake Michigan twenty miles away, presumably because he wanted me and my name-dropping to jump into it. Apparently sleeping with rank—or *aspiring* to sleep with rank—did not have its privileges.

The paramedic climbed into the ambulance and I went off in search of Pavlik. I found him talking to a man next to a car marked 'Inspector.' Since the car was red, I assumed it was the fire inspector.

When Pavlik saw me, he held up one finger. Either that meant I was to wait, or that I was Number One. I liked to think both.

Pavlik finished up and came over to me. 'This is going to take a while. Can I have a rain check?'

'You're invited for dinner anytime,' I said, my heart sinking just a bit. This despite the fact that Pavlik had about as good a reason for missing dinner as anyone I knew. I looked back at the burned remnants of Janalee's Place.

'That's not what I want the rain check for,' he murmured in my ear.

'Good thing,' I said, turning back to him. 'I'm a crappy cook.'

'Happily,' said Pavlik, 'I'm not. Next time dinner's at my house.'

Was this man perfect, or what? Dinner at his house. That meant no cooking, no cleaning and—most importantly—no competition from Frank.

I started up on my tiptoes to give Pavlik a quick kiss and then thought better of it. 'I suppose it's not proper to kiss the sheriff at a crime scene,' I said. 'Though I suppose this is really a fire scene not a cr—'

He leaned down to kiss me, maybe because he liked me or maybe because he wanted to shut me up. Either way, it worked for me. 'I'll call you tomorrow.'

'Perfect.' I started to walk away and then turned back. Often what Pavlik *didn't* say was more telling than what he did say. 'This isn't a crime scene, right? I mean, the fire was an accident.'

For the first time, I wondered why Pavlik had been called there. Fires weren't normally in his purview.

'I'll call you tomorrow,' was all he said.

EIGHT

When I got home, I nobly ignored Ingmar Bergman's *Through a Glass Darkly,* beckoning me from its DVD case on the coffee table. Instead, I did penance for my evil now-Amy-needs-a-job thoughts by settling onto the couch to go over Janalee's folders.

Disappointingly, the one entitled 'Competitive Strategies' was not LaRoche's master plan for conquering the coffee universe, but an old folder Janalee had stuffed full of every imaginable fact about Davy, including chronicling what appeared to be each bowel movement the colicky baby had ever had, when he held up his head the first time, the month, day and time he sat up, and the day he stood.

I had carefully preserved a box of growth charts, artwork and assembled memorabilia from Eric's childhood. The way Janalee was going, though, she would need a semi-trailer by the time Davy was grown. Setting aside the file to return to Janalee as quickly as humanly possible, I moved on to the other folders.

Happily, Janalee had paid the same attention to detail in planning the barista competition that she did to the care and feeding of Davy. Java Ho's event was designed to be a 'starter' competition and, much like a starter bra, the basics were there, but so was an expectation of further development.

The idea was to get our local *baristi* accustomed to competition, so they could go on to participate in sanctioned events put on by the Specialty Coffee Association of America and the United States Barista Competition. Lawyers and accountants have nothing on us as far as associations go.

Janalee had lined up the prescribed six judges—four of them sensory judges and two of them technical—and asked that they meet me at the convention center on Thursday morning. Her husband, Marvin, her notes said chirpily—assuming it was possible for ink to chirp— would be the head judge. That left me as master of ceremonies, which suited me just fine.

As far as I could tell, the competition should be fairly easy to manage. A piece of cake compared with the big events I'd been responsible for at First National. But then, as an exasperated coworker once told me, I obsessed more over a dinner party for half a dozen than a fireworks show for half a million. Made sense to me: five friends were more likely to complain than 500,000 strangers. It was just a fact of life. Besides, I was a lot more confident of my management skills than my cooking abilities...

'Uh-oh,' I said out loud, getting up off the couch. Frank, playing dead in front of the fireplace, raised his head a half inch off the floor to watch me run into the kitchen.

The bag from Schultz's was sitting on the counter where I'd left it while I preheated the broiler. I reached in and pulled out the bag o' halibut.

The fish was floating.

'Aren't you supposed to be on your backs?' I asked the fillets. I was recalling my earlier conversation with Amy.

To think we'd been standing in front of the seafood counter at Schultz's less than three hours ago, chatting about goldfish. And now the store Amy managed was gone, along with her job, perhaps. I assumed that Janalee would offer Amy something at a HotWired store, but would the rock barista take it?

With the exception of Amy at Janalee's Place, the HotWired staff members were as interchangeable as their surroundings. Not their fault, really. It was the way LaRoche wanted them. Uniform, efficient and faceless. Amy was anything but faceless, and I wasn't sure she would fit in anywhere but Janalee's.

Except Uncommon Grounds, of course.

I tossed the fish in the garbage and walked back into the living room, thinking about what made a place special. The point of differentiation. The people, right? In a coffeehouse, that would be the owners and employees who greeted you by name and knew what you drank. Made you feel at home. Or better than at home.

If we were going to beat HotWired, I thought as I stacked up Janalee's files, we needed to appeal to people's hearts, not their wallets. Our pockets just weren't deep enough to compete with LaRoche's free drink coupons. 'We *do* have big hearts, though,' I said out loud.

Frank snorted, giving me a momentary glimpse of one eye, and then went back to sleep. Cynic.

I would get an early start tomorrow. First I would check out the convention center so there wouldn't be any surprises on Thursday morning when I met with the judges. Then I would spend some time at Uncommon Grounds spreading good will. And force Caron to do likewise.

The remains of the Pinot Noir Pavlik had brought was sitting on the coffee table next to the DVD of *Through a Glass Darkly*. I had been about to pour us more wine when the call about the fire came in.

I picked up the bottle. Just enough left for a glass or two. I glanced over at the clock on the mantel. And just enough time. I poured the wine and slipped the DVD into the player.

DESPITE THE FACT I'd paired the wine with a sleeve of crackers and a can of spray cheese, I awoke famished the next morning. Go figure.

I decided to flip my itinerary and go to Uncommon Grounds first, before moving on to the convention center. The reason being free food, of course.

It was nearly eight thirty by the time I walked in the door, so I was surprised to see seven customers in line at the counter. Mindful of my resolution, I made sure to greet each person before I went behind the counter and dug out an almond poppy seed muffin.

'You *are* going to help, aren't you?' Caron demanded, as she poured a cup of coffee for a customer. 'I mean, someone besides yourself?'

'Of course,' I said, stuffing a piece of muffin in my mouth. 'Just needed a little nourishment first. A cup of coffee would help,' I said, eying the mug in Caron's hand.

'Don't even think about it,' the woman at the front of the line said. 'And don't you be putting any of your dirty pictures on it, either.' She snatched the cup from Caron and scuttled away to a corner table.

Mrs Doherty. The recipient of my one and only attempt at latte art. The woman had no imagination. Or, perhaps, too much of one. Either way, I wouldn't be winning her heart anytime soon. Best leave that one to Caron.

I turned to the next customer in line, a woman wearing a jacket over tennis whites. 'Dorothy—it's good to see you. Your usual, I presume?'

'I'd *prefer* Alice's usual,' the woman said, shaking her dark hair. It didn't move. Too much product.

'Alice's usual?' I asked, confused. 'I'm afraid I don't know—'

'Her name is Alice,' Caron hissed in my ear as she elbowed me out of the way. 'Not Dorothy.'

'But Dorothy is the one who wears tennis outfits,' I said, puzzled.

Caron rolled her eyes and started an espresso shot. 'Leagues started this week. Everyone is wearing tennis clothes.'

And this was *my* problem apparently. If they were all going to dress alike, they should have their names on their jerseys.

'Don't you have somewhere else to be?' Caron was trying to reach around me for a cup.

'I thought you wanted help,' I protested.

'Competent help.' Caron added hot water to the espresso for a café Americano. 'And why are you trying to suck up to the customers? You're not good at it.'

'That's true,' someone agreed from the back of the line.

'I liked her better when she was assigning seats,' another chimed in. Others were nodding in agreement.

'Hey, listen,' I said to the assemblage, 'I'm doing my best here.'

'Well, it's not good enough,' the Customer Formerly Known As Dorothy said. 'You know who you should hire? That Amy from Janalee's Place.'

'Did you hear there was a fire there last night?' Mrs Doherty piped up from her corner table.

'There was?' Caron looked sideways at me.

I nodded. 'It looked like a complete loss to me.'

'To you?' Caron echoed. 'How did you see it?'

Everybody stared at me.

'I...I drove by on my way here,' I said. I didn't need the whole store to know I'd gone there with Pavlik last night. 'I had heard about it on the news.'

'Yes,' Mrs Doherty agreed solemnly, 'that new girl on Channel Eight was talking about it.'

'Have you noticed how much weight she's gained?' Dorothy/Alice asked, carrying a bagel the size of a Buick to her table.

'I hear she's pregnant,' someone in the back contributed.

'But she's not married,' another gasped.

And off to the races we went from there. But at least they weren't gossiping about me.

I helped Caron whittle down the line and then made myself a latte for the road. 'I need to go to the convention center. Make sure everything is set for tomorrow.'

'Good idea,' Caron said, wiping a coffee ring off the condiment cart. 'But first, tell me: how did you really know about the fire?'

I shrugged. 'I was with Pavlik when he got the call,' I admitted.

'*With?*' Caron asked, a sly smile on her face.

'Not in that way,' I said. 'We were about to have dinner.'

'Well, I guess it's a start.' She sounded doubtful.

'He's cooking me dinner next time,' I said proudly.

'Cooking you dinner?' Now Caron was beaming like a proud mom. 'You know what *that* means.'

'That he's interested?' I asked.

'Even better,' she said, opening the door to usher me out. 'He's intelligent.'

She shut the door behind me.

THE BANNER ABOVE the convention center said: Welcome Travel Planners!!

Apparently the travel planners were no longer quite as welcome, though, because workers were undoing the ropes on each end of the banner. As a cluster of people smoking cigarettes watched, the banner was lowered to the ground. Presumably, by tomorrow it would be replaced by one that read: Welcome Java Ho!!

As I passed by the smokers, I thought about Sarah and her nicotine puffer. I hoped this time the fix would stick.

Inside, the big entrance lobby—dubbed the Grand Foyer—was quiet. Just the occasional travel planner scurrying out the big revolving door. When I reached the exhibit hall, though, it was another story.

Booths were being ripped apart, props and travel brochures packed up, tables and chairs folded and stacked, carpets yanked up. The blank walls and concrete floors left behind looked naked and a little embarrassed.

I found a man with a convention center name badge. He was doing his best to direct traffic. 'I'm sure you have your hands full, but I'm with Java Ho,' I told him.

He checked his clipboard. 'Your move-in isn't until tomorrow a.m.'

'Right,' I said. 'But I'm running the barista competition and I was hoping I could see where we're going to be.'

He pointed toward the far end of the huge room. 'We have you down there. We'll bring a temporary wall across to separate you from the exhibitors.'

'Is it a solid wall? How will people get in?'

'There's a door in the wall, plus there's a separate exit into the corridor by the bar.'

'Perfect,' I said. I made a note to have a couple of signs made so people could find us.

'Do you happen to have the floor plan for the competition area there?' I asked, peering over his shoulder at his clipboard. I didn't want to wear out my welcome, but I wanted to make sure Janalee's instructions had been passed on.

The man—his name tag said 'Raymond'—paged through the sheaf of papers and pulled one out.

'Here it is,' he said, handing it to me distractedly as he tried to keep tabs on the activity around us.

I looked over the paper. A stage with six six-foot tables for the competitors. Two would form an 'L' for each of the three work stations. Electrical outlets for the espresso machines, grinders, blenders and mini-refrigerators. Hand-held wireless microphone for me, so I could move around. A six-foot table for judges on the floor in front of the stage. Bleachers beyond that. Dividers behind the stage to hide the supplies and staging area. Janalee had thought of everything. Almost.

'Just one thing,' I said. 'Could I get another six-foot table on the stage? I'll need it for trophies.'

Raymond took the floor plan and looked it over. 'Would an eight-footer work? We're short on sixes.'

I nodded.

He made a note. 'Anything else?'

Raymond was looking across the hall at a twelve-foot palm tree that was swaying—and not in the wind. As we watched, the tree crashed to the ground, scattering paper palm fronds all the way from 'See France!' to 'Experience Tokyo!' and back.

'You go ahead,' I said to Raymond. 'And thank you,' I called after him as he hurried away.

Raymond waved back. The man was awfully patient considering everything he had going on.

I hoped Sarah would be likewise tomorrow.

But then, I also prayed for world peace every night, and so far that wasn't going very well, either.

NINE

WHEN I ARRIVED AT the convention center at eight a.m. the next morning, I found Sarah already in the exhibit hall, which was in the process of being transformed into a caffeinated paradise. By the time all the vendors got in there, you wouldn't have to drink the stuff, you could just inhale it.

'You're here bright and early,' I greeted her cheerily.

Sarah pointed at herself. 'See this face? I haven't had a cigarette for nearly seventy-two hours. This may be early, but it sure as hell isn't bright.'

'OK,' I conceded, 'but *I'm* feeling bright.'

'Why? Because Amy's store burned down Tuesday so she needs a job?'

I gasped and grabbed her arm. 'How can you say something like that?'

Sarah snorted. 'Yeah, like you didn't think it.'

'How did you…I mean, why would you think…'

She turned around and faced me full on. 'Because *I* thought of it.'

'And just because you think evil thoughts,' I said indignantly, 'you assume that I do, too?'

'I don't assume. I know.' She waggled her head and laid her hand on my shoulder. 'Maggy, Maggy, Maggy. Don't you know that you are simply me, reflected in a socially acceptable mirror?'

Talk about through a glass darkly. My face must have reflected my horror, because Sarah cackled and dropped her hand. 'Deny it all you want, Maggy, but I say the things that you only think.'

Damn right, and that's the way it should stay. I opened my mouth to tell her just that—in a socially acceptable way, of course—but Sarah was already running after a woman pushing an espresso machine on a dolly.

'What did you do, get lost getting out of bed this morning?' Sarah screamed at her. 'You have booth four-fifty, not four-sixty, and you were supposed to be set up by eight…'

I put my hands over my ears and retreated to the competition room, repeating, 'I am not Sarah, I am a good person. I am not Sarah, I am a good person,' until her voice faded.

Didn't the fact that I was contemplating buying Sarah a pack of cigarettes just to shut her up prove her point, though?

'WE HAVE EIGHTEEN competitors,' I explained to the assembled judges, 'so we won't need to do both semi-finals and finals after the first round. We should be able to winnow the group down to six finalists so we can finish on Saturday. Make sense?'

The two technical judges, the accountants of the coffee world, just looked at me.

One of the sensory judges, a bleached blonde, who must have been a bombshell at one time, nodded in agreement. 'God, yes. That way we can enjoy Sunday.'

The prissy woman standing next to her gave her a sidelong glance. 'You mean you can enjoy partying on Saturday night and sleep in on Sunday, don't you, Barbara?'

Barbara raised her eyebrows. 'I don't think we want to start talking about sleeping arrangements, do you, Priscilla?' She looked pointedly from Priscilla to one of the technical judges.

Priscilla turned red. The tech judge just glared at Barbara and pushed his glasses up on his nose, using what Eric would have called his 'swear finger'.

Geez, what next? Spin the bottle? Short-sheeting beds? And these were the judges I was dealing with. This really did have 'reality show' written all over it.

I cleared my throat. 'The competitors will practice today and get acquainted with the equipment. Then the competition starts tomorrow afternoon at one. The finals are Saturday morning at ten. Everybody got it?'

I took the muted muttering as acquiescence. 'One other thing, there will be television coverage—' the judges perked up— 'by the local cable station.' Oops, lost them again. They filed out before I could go any further.

Just as well. I didn't want any of them stealing my idea. As I stacked up my papers, there was a muffled knock on the temporary wall that separated the competition room from the exhibit hall. The wall was padded— something that might come in handy by the time this was all over.

'Knock, knock.' Marvin LaRoche stuck his head in.

I thought about giving him a dressing down for not being in time for the judges' briefing, but, intent on not being Sarah's dark reflection, I settled for: 'How's our chief judge this morning?'

'Fantastic, thank you.' LaRoche swept into the room and sat on a corner of the table. He was wearing a suit and tie, but then LaRoche always wore a suit and tie. Even at HotWired. 'We're going to have a fabulous function. And are plans proceeding for the coming competition?'

'Of course,' I said. 'What about your opening address? A spellbinding speech, I suspect?' Hey, I could be alliteratively effusive, too.

Not that LaRoche noticed. 'I truly believe so,' he said, growing serious. 'The subject of my keynote is cultivating creativity in coffee.'

'Compelling,' I offered.

'Crucial,' he agreed.

Enough of these games. 'All alliteration aside, Marvin...' He looked at me blankly, so I didn't bother to explain. 'As I told the rest of the judges, the competition starts at one tomorrow, with the finals at ten on Saturday. I've confirmed with them that we can do it in two stages instead of three.' I'd also confirmed that the judges were a bunch of loonies.

'Perfect,' he said, standing up and preparing to leave. 'I'll put it on my calendar.'

'Oh, wait,' I said, pawing through the folders in front of me. 'Janalee accidentally gave me one of her personal files, could you give it back to her?'

LaRoche looked momentarily put-out at being asked to be an errand boy. Then he must have remembered he was both fantastic and fabulous.

'Of course,' he said, beaming broadly. 'Happy to have an excuse to see my lovely bride.'

As he left, I had to wonder: if Sarah was *my* dark reflection, whose dark side was LaRoche?

THE NEXT ARRIVALS to the competition room were The Milkman and L'Cafe in that order. This was a problem because The Milkman had all the perishable milk, cream and dairy products for the event, and L'Cafe had all the equipment. Including the refrigerators—big ones for backstage and three minis for the workstations on stage.

We finally got it straightened out and by the time the entrants arrived, the three competition stations were set up. Each work area had an identical espresso machine, grinder and blender, plus staples like a knock box for the grounds, trash can and the mini-refrigerator, of course. Everything else had to be provided by the participants, from mood music for their fifteen-minute presentation, right down to the espresso itself.

Janalee had arranged for the entrants to arrive in shifts of three to prepare, and I was surprised to see Amy in the first group.

'Are you going to be able to compete?' I asked her.

She raised her bandaged right hand. 'Luckily, I'm a lefty.'

'Still, frothing takes two hands, and even holding back the foam when you're pouring the milk for a cappuccino…?'

'I know it's a long shot.' She put down the basket of china she was carrying on her arm. 'But I'll do my best. That will have to be enough.'

I liked this woman. 'It's all anyone could ask—more, given the circumstances. Any word yet on the cause of the fire?'

I had asked Pavlik the same question via cell phone message, but hadn't gotten an answer. I suspected he was ducking the subject, but hadn't a clue why. The most logical reason, of course, was that he didn't know. Maybe the fire chief had kicked him out after I left and Pavlik didn't want to admit it. Maybe there was some sort of turf war going on between the fire department and the sheriff's office. Maybe I watched too much TV.

Amy shrugged. 'Not that I've heard. The place is a total loss, though.'

'Do you think Marvin and Janalee will rebuild?' Evil thoughts, unbidden, were starting to run through my mind. Even if they did rebuild, Amy could be displaced for months.

'If they do, Marvin says it will be a HotWired,' Amy said. 'Not Janalee's Place.'

'Of course not,' I said, helping her unpack her supplies. 'Janalee's Place had too much personality for...' I slapped my mouth closed. Depending on how much of a cynic you are, you could say I shut up because I didn't want to bad-mouth my competition. You could also say it was because I didn't want to offend my prospective barista, Amy.

Either way, I had the sense to shut my mouth.

Still, Amy's eyes narrowed and her lips pursed. Watching, I was afraid her lip piercings were going to lock up like car fenders in a crash. And if that happened, whom would I call for help? A doctor? A dentist? A jeweler?

Amy said, 'Your partner talked to me a while back about coming to work for you.'

'Yesss.' Uh-oh, the woman had seen right through me. She knew that I was nosing around.

'Are you still interested?'

'Yes!' I said, perhaps a little too eagerly. I tried to soften it a bit. 'But I wouldn't ask you to leave HotWired when Janalee is already dealing with the fire.' Way to go, Maggy. Make the woman feel guilty for jumping ship. *That's* going to win you a barista.

But Amy looked like she had come to a decision. 'Don't worry about that. I need to leave. It was over before the fire ever began.'

'Well, if you're sure. When do you think you could start?' Maybe I could hire Amy on the spot and she could compete for Uncommon Grounds—win one for the home team. Of course, then I would need to step down from my position so I couldn't be accused of favoritism or fixing the competition. Talk about a win-win situation.

Amy opened up her mouth to answer my question, but all I could hear was screaming baby. Probably wet, screaming baby.

Janalee had arrived. And not only did she have Davy, but she was pushing a wheeled cart.

Surprised, I glanced down at my list of competitors. 'Are you participating, Janalee? I don't see you on my list.'

Janalee unslung Davy and set him down on the floor. 'We had a last-minute dropout, and I thought, why not?'

Why not? The more the merrier. Her husband was the head judge and she was competing against her best barista. Yet another reason Amy should come to work for Caron and me. 'Will we have a conflict with Marvin judging?'

Janalee waved it off. 'The head judge doesn't actually do any scoring, as you no doubt saw in the information I gave you.'

'I did, but I think I also saw that he could be called on to break a tie.'

'Davy, sweetie, I'm sure they don't have your soy milk in there. We have to keep the door shut or the other milk will curdle.' She looked at us from the floor, where she'd settled. 'He's just fascinated with the light in the refrigerator.'

'Aren't we all,' I muttered.

I must have sounded a wee bit too flippant for Davy's taste. The baby threw me a dirty look and crawled back to his mother.

I shivered. It was like there was a tiny adult hiding behind those too-wise brown eyes. Pull back the curtain, and the Wizard of Oz is working the ropes.

'But back to the judging,' Janalee was saying. 'Marvin would only be called upon in the event of a tie in the finals. I'm sure that I won't make the finals, though I do wonder what we will do if our star barista does.' She smiled over at Amy.

Amy smiled back and held up her bandaged hand. 'Not much chance of that, I think.'

A crash out in the exhibit hall made us all turn. It was followed by a string of expletives that could come from only one source: Sarah.

Janalee put her hands over Davy's ears, as the ruckus in the next room continued. I looked at Amy, my new—almost—employee. What a perfect opportunity for her to show some initiative.

'I suppose someone should see what's going on,' I said leadingly.

Amy just held up her gauze-covered paw.

Janalee looked up from where she was still forming a protective barrier over Davy's ears. 'I would, but...'

Another crash, and then another, and another. Each one getting a little faster. 'It sounds like a giant game of dominoes,' I said.

The thought struck all three of us at the same time. 'The booth dividers.'

We ran out in time to see the final five go down. The last one fell with a gigantic 'thwopp' followed by silence. In the convention hall, people stood motionless, frozen where they were when the walls came tumbling down. EarthBean's Levitt Fredericks was holding a poster he'd been about to pin to a wall that was no longer there. A union workman who had been taping down the carpet was now partly covered by that wall. A hapless smoothie machine vendor was sprawled over the first of the giant dominoes. The point of origin, no doubt.

And then there was Sarah. She stood about a foot away from the top of the last wall that had fallen. A foot away from being snuffed out.

Like she had read my mind, Sarah reached in her pocket and pulled out a bent cigarette. Picking the lint off it, she stuck it in her mouth and looked around for a light.

I found one for her.

Better she smoke it than shove it down someone's throat.

TEN

BY THE TIME THE BARS opened for the welcoming cocktail party, there was a line a block long at each. The people at the very front of each line looked like exhibitors.

In other words, Sarah's people.

She and I stood behind one of the bars. She was vodka neat. I had a glass of Pinot Noir.

'Enjoying your Java Ho experience so far?' I asked pleasantly. 'Glad you volunteered?'

The noise she made was somewhere between a plaintive cry and a snarl.

'I have to admit,' I continued, 'I'm having a grand time. Hey, there's Caron.'

I waved my partner over and had the bartender get her a Scotch. The guy in the front of the line—the smoothie vendor who had caused the catastrophe in the exhibit hall—started to give me a dirty look and then saw Sarah next to me. He slunk off without his drink.

'A toast,' I said, holding up my glass. 'To Sarah, who admittedly had one day from hell, but only had half a cigarette in response.'

We clanged glasses.

Sarah pulled the unsmoked part of the cigarette out of her pocket. 'I'm keeping it. God knows, with this band of idiots I may need it.'

'Thanks for sending the photo, Maggy,' Caron said.

Sarah looked at me.

I shrugged. 'I sent her a picture via cellphone. Why should she miss all the fun?'

Sarah started to say something, but then gave it up. The poor thing seemed exhausted.

Not me, though. I was psyched. 'I have another toast. Raise those glasses.'

They did, and I said, 'To Amy, whose last name is Caprese. Our new barista.'

Caron gasped. 'You did it!'

Sarah was considerably less effusive. 'Did what? Burn down their store, so you could steal their barista?'

She said it so loud that two older women in the bar line looked at us and started to whisper.

I elbowed Sarah. 'Shh. Rumors spread like crazy at one of these things.'

'Rumors? You mean like the one about the giant domino game in the exhibit hall?'

'That is not a rumor, it's fact.'

'Yeah, and because you mentioned dominoes, some smart-ass cut big black dots out of construction paper,' Sarah said. 'They were taping them on the dividers so they looked like domino tiles when I caught them.'

Actually, I thought that was pretty funny. I didn't think the vendors had it in them. 'Mutiny,' I declared. 'Did you have them keelhauled?'

'I would have if I'd known what the hell it was,' Sarah muttered.

'The original meaning is exactly what it sounds like,' Caron told her. 'Being hauled or towed under the keel of a boat. It was used as a punishment before—'

Sarah interrupted. 'Let's cut to the chase. Did it drown them? Or just waterlog them?' She sounded like she preferred Door Number One.

Caron just shook her head and turned to me. 'Now, tell me the truth, is Amy really going to work for us?'

'Did Maggy *really* go over to the dark side?' Sarah parroted into her drink.

I elbowed her again. 'I did *not* offer Amy a job.'

Caron looked crushed. 'But you just said…'

'Amy asked *me* if we still wanted her, and I said yes.'

Caron hugged me so enthusiastically she spilled her drink down my back.

As I extricated myself, I said, 'So I didn't have to go over to "the dark side", as you put it, Sarah. I just had to be there.'

'Ingratiate yourself, you mean.' Sarah said. 'Suck up. Be her new best friend. Whatever you want to call it, it's still manipulation.'

'It is not manipulation—'

I was interrupted by Caron. 'There's Amy now, with Janalee. Does Janalee know?'

'I doubt it,' said Sarah. 'They're looking pretty tight.'

I turned to see. Amy was holding Davy and Janalee appeared to be teasing her about something. Maybe I had jumped the gun in announcing it to Caron. 'I'm sure Amy hasn't said a word to anyone and neither should we. She and I were just starting to discuss it when we were interrupted.'

Caron was looking worried. 'Well, will you firm it up with her tomorrow?'

'Firm up what?' Kate McNamara had just sidled in. With the four of us and the bartender behind the bar it was starting to get a tad cozy.

'Where's your camera man?' I asked her to change the subject. 'LaRoche is going to start speaking in about fifteen minutes.'

Elementary convention-planning: give everyone a chance to get well-lubricated before you subject them to a keynote address.

'My *crew* is bringing the equipment in,' Kate said loftily. 'You don't need to worry about a thing except getting me a drink.'

I worried about many things. Getting Kate a drink was not one of them. Nonetheless, I tapped the bartender on the shoulder.

'Listen,' he said, when he swiveled around, 'the people at the front of the line—' he poked his thumb over his shoulder— 'are about to climb over the bar and kill us all with their bare hands. I'll get you one more, and then you have to get out from behind here.'

'Deal,' I said. 'I'll have another Pinot Noir, and we'll need another Scotch, a vodka, neat, and...what are you drinking, Kate?'

'Captain Morgan Private and Diet Coke.'

The bartender looked heavenward and turned back to his customers, the two old ladies who had overheard Sarah accuse me of burning down Janalee's Place.

'Oh, but get the ladies their drinks first,' I called over to him. 'On our tab.'

I smiled at the two women, and they smiled back. I turned to Caron and Sarah. 'Listen, once the drinks come, Kate and I are going to go set up.'

'We are?' Kate said, taking the drink the bartender held out to her. 'Did I say I needed your help?'

'You do know Marvin LaRoche, right?' I asked her dryly.

'Yes, as you're well aware. You were there in his office—'

'Then you also know you need all the help you can get,' Caron interrupted, nodding wisely. 'Maybe I should come, too.'

'Don't even think about it, Egan,' Sarah said. 'The three of you are not going to take off and stick me with the drink tab.'

'Of course not.' I waved at the bartender. 'Can you put this on Marvin LaRoche's tab?' I asked him. When he hesitated, I added, 'And give yourself a thirty percent tip?'

He perked right up. 'Done.'

Caron was shaking her head. 'You get vindictive when you get liquored-up.'

'Liquored-up on one glass of wine?' Kate asked in a disparaging tone. 'What would you do if you had a real drink?'

'Burn down the Place?' Sarah suggested.

'Will you all shut up about fire,' I said, glancing around for the two old ladies. 'And I don't think someone who has been drinking rum and Cokes since she was fifteen, Kate, should talk about *real* drinks.'

Kate took a slug of her drink and nearly spit it out. 'What in the world is this?'

'House brand. You ordered spiced rum—premium, no less—at a porta-bar in a convention center. Did you really think they'd have it?'

'I didn't mean the rum, I meant the Coke. This is Diet Pepsi!'

'What's wrong with that?' Caron demanded. 'I like Pepsi. Coca Cola is—'

'Forgive me for interrupting the Pepsi challenge,' Sarah said, 'but is that your cameraman—and I use the term advisedly—Kate?'

We followed where she was pointing. At the entrance of the hall stood a boy who looked to be fourteen.

'That camera is bigger than he is,' Caron said. 'Someone help him before it crushes the poor boy.'

'Look,' Sarah contributed, 'his knees are starting to buckle.'

'Have you people no compassion, no empathy?' I demanded, putting my wineglass on the bar. 'That kid goes down, it's the end of my TV show.'

'*Our* TV show.' Kate joined me to elbow our way through the crowd.

The camera kid was setting the camera down when we reached him. He was maybe five-two, with a freckled face, glasses and close-cropped blond hair.

He straightened up when he saw us and stuck out his hand to Kate. 'Kate, good to see you again. We're nearly set up here. Jill just ran back to the truck to get a light stand.'

He turned to me. 'And you must be our emcee, Maggy Thorsen.'

'Maggy, meet Jack,' Kate said, apparently reminded of her manners by a kid who had enough for both of them.

He smiled patiently. 'Actually, my name is Jerome. Kate just finds it easier to remember Jack and Jill.'

'I see,' I said, glancing at Kate, who was scanning some notes. 'Jerome and Jill just doesn't have the same ring, does it?'

'Apparently not,' Jerome/Jack said, the same patient smile on his face.

This kid was more mature than I would ever be. Combine that with the extremely short hair, the straight-ahead I'll-take-whatever-life-sends-me gaze, and it seemed all too familiar.

My brother had that look—the look of a kid who had fought a battle someone his age shouldn't have to fight.

'Ready, Maggy?' Kate was saying.

'I'm sorry—what?'

'I asked if you were ready,' Kate repeated impatiently. 'Marvin's getting miked-up.'

I turned. He was indeed clipping a Lavaliere microphone to his lapel at the direction of a union engineer. LaRoche sported a different dark suit than he'd had on earlier. His accessories included cufflinks, a school tie and a wife and baby at his right shoulder and one step back. There was no wet spot on either Janalee or Davy. I assumed rubber pants were part of Davy's formal-wear.

'LaRoach is certainly ready.' I said.

'Wait.' Kate was checking her notes again. 'I thought it was pronounced *LaRoshay*. Jill?' She looked around wildly. 'Where is she? How long can it take to go to the truck?'

'Here I am, Kate.' A girl, presumably Jill, ran up, winded. She was taller than Jerome by six inches and was holding the stand and base for a light. 'What do you need?'

'Didn't you confirm the name was *LaRoshay,* not *LaRoach?*' Kate started in.

'Wait, wait, wait,' I said, before my contrariness got the kid into any more trouble. 'He does pronounce it with the "shay".' I explained about Marvin's pronunciation of his name, versus the rest of the family. 'This is his convention, so we'd best go with his version.'

Jill grinned gratefully at me. 'Glad I had it right. I'm going to talk to the convention's AV guys and get a feed from their audio.' She took off.

I had to give her credit for not being cowed by Kate. I had a feeling these kids were going to be just fine.

'We just have the one camera tonight,' Jerome was saying, 'but we'll have three for the barista competition.'

'Good,' Kate said, 'that means the second and third cameras can—'

'Is this thing on?' LaRoche's voice boomed out over the sound system.

Our execs at First National had thought it necessary to start speeches like that, after paying professionals big bucks to make sure the microphones were indeed on.

'Just start your speech,' I muttered. 'If it isn't working, you'll find out soon enough.'

Sadly for those of us in the audience, the microphone was working just fine.

First, we were subjected to ten minutes of self-aggrandizing.

'He's not going to whip out the home movies, is he?' Kate leaned over and asked at one point.

'Just so he doesn't whip out something else,' I whispered back.

'Onan the Barbarian,' Kate snickered softly.

I, on the other hand, laughed out loud. Snorted, even.

LaRoche, who had just explained how he'd taken a thousand dollars' seed money and grown it into a chain of twenty HotWired stores 'and counting', peered into the crowd. I stepped into the shadows behind Jerome, who was taping.

'Apparently LaRoche has conveniently forgotten his wife's contribution of an already successful coffeehouse,' I muttered more to myself than to Jerome. 'The man wouldn't know a porta-filter from a Porta-Potty without Janalee.'

LaRoche's partner in life and love had stepped even farther back on the stage, apparently trying to become one with the curtain. Given that she was wearing a black suit and the curtains were black, I figured she had a shot at it as long as she and Davy didn't topple off the stage backwards.

Having discounted his wife and demeaned every coffeehouse owner who was happy to own one or two stores, LaRoche went on to call socially conscious efforts like Fair Trade and shade-grown coffee 'fiscally *un*conscious'.

An angry buzz started amongst Levitt Fredericks' EarthBean group. By the time LaRoche had gotten around to suggesting coffeehouse owners buy their own roasting operations and dairies to 'cut out the middleman, and retain more of the income', the buzz had turned to a roar. He had alienated 'the middlemen' along with nearly everyone else in the room.

When he ended with: '...and that is how you, too, can cultivate creativity and profits,' he obviously expected applause.

'Guess we know what the sound of one hand clapping is,' a voice in my ear said. Sarah had emerged from behind the bar. She nodded toward Janalee, who was doing her best to applaud while juggling Davy. Amy was in the EarthBean camp and didn't even try.

'This is embarrassing,' Jerome said, still keeping his eye to the camera lens. 'Shouldn't you start the applause just to get him off stage?'

LaRoche was standing next to the lectern with a big grin on his face.

'Can't,' I said. 'I'm an independent coffeehouse owner. If I applaud, it means I agree with him.'

'And you don't?' Jerome twisted his head around and asked.

'There's money to be made in coffee, but not at the expense of the children in the fields, or the growers, or the roasters. Or the earth, itself, for that matter.'

Jerome smiled and turned back to the camera.

'C'mon, Maggy, clap,' Sarah said. If Jerome was the angel at my right shoulder, Sarah was the devil at my left. 'It isn't like you haven't been the shill in the audience before.'

She was right. At First National I would stand in the back and clap or laugh in all the right places to kick-start the audience for the execs.

'I don't have to be anyone's shill anymore,' I said to Sarah, a little too loud in the quiet room.

But in that second, someone on the convention staff must have had a brainstorm, because the sound system kicked in and Springsteen's 'Born in the USA' enveloped the room.

Under patriotic cover, LaRoche stepped down from the stage and started chatting up the front row. Janalee hesitated and then disappeared behind the curtains.

The rest of us headed for the bars.

ELEVEN

THE NEXT MORNING I had a bit of a headache from closing the bar the night before. The talk had been all about the Talk and how could I miss a second of that? Unsurprisingly, the consensus was that LaRoche should be exterminated.

Or maybe asphyxiated. That would take care of him, I thought as I ran the blue haze gauntlet outside the convention center. The smokers had again formed a knot outside the front door. No surprise there, but I was happy to see Sarah hadn't joined them.

I was also happy to see that there were no life-size domino games going on in the exhibit hall. Indeed, by the standards of the day before, Java Ho was looking almost tame.

How Sarah had squeezed nearly five hundred vendors on the exhibition floor, I didn't know. Most of them were handing out free caffeine in various forms: lattes, cappuccinos, mochas, smoothies, hyper-charged caffeine shots and colas. People already were bouncing off the walls. It was little wonder that everyone spent the nights in the bar. Who could sleep?

As I passed through the hall on the way to the competition room, I saw Levitt Fredericks. 'The EarthBean booth looks good, Levitt. No damage from the little mishap yesterday?'

'Mishap?' Levitt uncoiled himself from a chair and stood up, always the southern gentleman. 'I swear, Miss Maggy, you have an exceptional gift for the understatement.'

'Why thank you, Mr Levitt,' I said with a sweeping curtsy. 'I'm trying to become a cup-half-full kind of person.'

'Good luck to you on that,' he said, getting somber. 'The way things are going, the cups of most everyone in the coffee industry are going to be half empty. Or worse.'

'You mean LaRoche's speech?' I asked, catching sight of Janalee approaching. Every few feet someone stopped her to talk. I was glad to see people weren't blaming her for last night. 'You know he doesn't speak for the rest of us.'

The tall gray-haired man nodded. 'Of course, my dear. And not to worry, EarthBean has taken its share of shots over the years. No, it's the industry in general I worry about. Every man for them—'

'I'm sorry to interrupt.' Janalee had finally made it to us. She was without baby, for once.

'Not at all, Janalee. Are you OK?'

She didn't look OK. She looked like crap.

Seeing it, Levitt took her hand and led her over to his chair. 'Janalee, my dear, sit down. I hope you're not upset by last night.'

'Last night?' Janalee looked up at him blankly. 'Oh, you mean Marvin's speech. No, no—that was just Marvin being...Marvin. I know you understand.'

'Of course, of course.' Levitt patted her hand. 'Then whatever has you so disturbed?'

Janalee leaned forward in her seat and looked from me to Levitt and back again.

'Janalee's Place,' she said softly. 'Apparently someone burned it down on purpose. Who in the world would gain from starting the fire?'

She said the last in a hushed tone, but her words seemed to reverberate in the big hall. Fire, fire, fire...

The two old ladies from the bar last night passed by and glanced at us and then quickly away.

Now, *I* knew that I didn't burn down Janalee's Place. So why did I feel so guilty?

DESPITE THE NEWS ABOUT the fire, both Janalee and Amy still took part in the barista competition. By the time the audience had settled in, the stage was set and the judges and cameras were in place.

Jerome had positioned the three cameras so one was on the particular barista who was competing, the second moved between the judges and the audience and the third was on me.

And that suited me just fine.

'Welcome to the Second Annual Java Ho Barista Competition,' I said into the microphone.

The crowd burst into wild applause.

Already, I was one up on LaRoche.

Further buoying me was the fact that Sophie Daystrom and Henry Wested—my once and, I hoped, future customers—were seated front row center. Maybe they did still love me and Uncommon Grounds. *Or* maybe they were there to support Amy and Janalee from Hot-Wired.

I tried not to let the thought throw me off stride.

'Each competitor today will have a chance to prepare an espresso, a cappuccino and a signature drink for each of our esteemed judges. They will be scored on taste, presentation and technical skills. All drinks must contain espresso, of course, but none can contain alcohol.'

I waved down the boos and smiled into the camera. I was liking this emcee stuff.

'The top six point-scorers will come back for the finals tomorrow morning to vie for this trophy.' I lifted the first-place trophy, ostensibly to show the crowd, but more to mug for the camera.

The bronze sculpture was supposed to be steam in the form of a barista, rising from a cup. But now, as I looked at it a little more closely, I realized...

'She's naked,' Sophie Daystrom exclaimed loudly from the front row.

'Shouldn't she at least have an apron on?' Henry asked in what he seemed to think was a whisper. 'A *big* one?'

I couldn't help it, I laughed. Then the whole audience laughed.

I think we had a hit on our hands.

JANALEE AND BARISTAS from Java the Hut and Bean There comprised the first trio of contestants.

'Isn't Java the Hut in the UK?' George, the technical judge who was *not* sleeping with Priscilla, asked as the Java the Hut barista, a young man named Mitchell, wheeled a cart with his supplies onstage.

'This is a different place,' I said, handing him a technical score sheet. 'Somewhere near Cincinnati, I think.'

When we were trying to come up with a name for our own coffeehouse, I'd learned that no matter how clever you thought your name was, someone already had come up with it.

'Is that legal?' Priscilla asked from the judges' table. While the technical judges roamed, looking for violations, the sensory judges got to sit down and be waited on.

'Don't know.' I gave Priscilla a sensory score sheet. 'It probably depends on trademarks and market areas and all that jazz.'

The judges had turned their attention to their score sheets, so I turned my microphone back on.

'Each of our contestants will have fifteen minutes to prepare their workstation, fifteen minutes to create their drinks, and fifteen minutes to clean up,' I told the crowd. 'Throughout that forty-five minutes, two of our judges will score the barista on his or her technical skills. Things like using the equipment properly and keeping the work area clean.'

Mitchell promptly knocked over the bag of coffee beans on his cart, sending them cascading on to the floor.

'Not to worry,' I said. 'The two technical scores are averaged together and added to all four sensory scores.'

I turned to make eye contact—or lens contact—with the camera. I was trying to treat it as a member of the audience. A very important member of the audience.

'The presentation, smell and taste of the drink itself, is more important than a few coffee beans on the floor.' I gestured grandly toward Mitchell and his beans.

Henry and Sophie applauded wildly. I smiled down at them. I liked having shills of my very own.

'Are you ready?' I asked Mitchell.

Having corralled most of his beans, he was standing next to his cart, waiting for my signal to start setting up. He nodded nervously in response to my question.

'Begin.' I clicked the stopwatch as Mitchell began to unload his cart.

'As you can see,' I explained, 'the competitors are responsible for bringing their own beans, as well as the drink ingredients.'

Mitchell was frantically shoving milk and cream into the mini-fridge. I wasn't sure why he was in such a hurry. He still had fourteen minutes of prep time.

'They also bring their own china, napkins and any decorations they might use,' I continued. 'Even ice—' Mitchell looked up from the table where he had been arranging his china— 'is the responsibility of the individual contestant.'

Mitchell pivoted with a yelp and raced offstage.

'Happily,' I said as I watched him run off, 'each contestant has this time to make sure he or she has everything they need. After this fifteen minutes—' Mitchell came skidding around the corner with an ice bucket— 'we will reset the clock for another fifteen minutes.'

I accidentally glanced down at Henry and Sophie. Apparently thinking it was their cue, they applauded.

I cleared my throat. 'Thank you. During that quarter hour, the contestant will prepare twelve drinks.'

'Oh, my Lord,' Sophie gasped. 'Twelve drinks?'

I couldn't help it: I looked at her.

Henry clapped.

Mae West was wrong. Too much of a good thing is *not* wonderful.

'Yes, twelve drinks in just fifteen minutes,' I said. 'First four espressos—one for each of the four sensory judges. Then, four cappuccinos. And finally, four of the barista's specialty drink.'

I could just *feel* Sophie and Henry staring up at me, their hands poised to applaud. I willed myself not to look.

'Each contestant also brings music to be played during his or her performance. Do we have the music queued?'

Because the convention center was a unionized facility, their tech people had to handle the music. The woman in charge of the CD deck nodded. That would probably cost LaRoche a cool fifty bucks. I stifled the impulse to ask her another question to up the ante.

Instead, I turned to look at Mitchell. He was standing to attention behind his work table. A bead of sweat trickled down his temple.

'Each barista will explain what he or she is doing as he or she is doing it.' I was starting to get tangled up in my gender-specific pronouns. Better switch to names. 'Mitchell will first introduce himself, and then begin.'

'Remember,' I went on, 'this barista is not only responsible for creating twelve exquisite drinks, but also for the table-setting and presentation to the judges. All this, while keeping his workstation perfectly orderly and clean. And all—' I paused for effect— 'in just fifteen minutes.'

I turned dramatically to the camera. 'Will this barista stand the test?' I boomed in my best reality-show voice.

There was a thud behind me, accompanied by the sound of breaking china.

'He's dead,' Sophie screamed.

I looked at her.

Henry applauded.

POOR MITCHELL opted out, even after we'd revived him.

'Maybe I shouldn't have been so dramatic,' I moaned to Kate as we took the equivalent of a TV time-out.

'Are you kidding?' Kate had a huge grin on her face. 'You were perfect. *He* was perfect.'

'He was unconscious, Kate.'

'Yes, and even before that. The sweat. The deer-in-the-headlights look when he forgot the ice. *Great* TV.' She pumped her fist in the air.

She was right, it *was* great TV. It was also the humiliation of a human being. I pointed that out.

'I know,' she said delightedly. 'Thank God we got releases.'

'We will *not* use that footage if he objects,' I said.

'Says who?' Kate demanded.

'Says me.'

'Oh, yeah?'

'Yeah.'

'Or what?'

'I'll tell you what—'

This mature exchange was interrupted by Jill. 'They've cleaned up the stage. Do you want us to start taping again?'

'Start taping?' Kate squawked. 'You mean you didn't tape the whole—'

I didn't wait to hear any more.

'OK,' I said, picking up my microphone. 'Let's get this show back on the road.'

I stepped out onstage. 'First, let me give you an update. Mitchell is going to be just fine,' I said. 'He passed out—'

'Probably low blood sugar,' Sophie offered up from the front row.

'More likely too much coffee,' Henry countered.

'*Whatever* it was,' I said pointedly, 'Mitchell is OK now. And the show must go on. Please help me welcome our next contestant: Janalee LaRoche of HotWired.'

Despite the fact she was married to LaRoche—or maybe in sympathy for the fact—Janalee got a big hand. Amy was watching from the audience with Davy on her lap. I assumed she and Janalee would change custody when Amy competed.

Even with the shock of recently finding out her store had been torched, not to mention having the barista before her hit the floor, Janalee was the consummate professional.

'As you see,' she told the crowd twenty-eight minutes later, as she spooned froth on the top of her final specialty drink, 'I've used fresh orange zest and that, combined with the espresso and heavy cream of my drink, brings back memories of the ice cream pops of our youth. I've taken great pains to make sure that while the espresso is the base of the drink, it doesn't overpower the more delicate cream and orange flavors.'

'I see you've chosen a mug rather than the more delicate bone china for your presentation,' I said, doing my part as both emcee and interviewer. 'Is there a reason for that?'

'This is not a delicate drink,' she said, placing a curl of orange peel on the top of the froth. 'It's a playful drink and that's the way I wanted to display it. Hence—' she placed a Popsicle stick in the cup as a stirrer and moved the drink to the presentation table with a flourish— *'voila.'*

The crowd applauded wildly.

Even without my looking at Henry and Sophie.

IT WAS HALFTIME of the competition and things were going smoothly. Better than smoothly.

'Wow,' I said, as Antonio re-supplied the competitors for the second half, 'people are really into this. I thought they were going to take my head off when I said we were going to break.'

'Everyone certainly needed it,' Antonio said, looking up from his clipboard. 'The refrigerators had to be restocked, and the judges also seemed to need to rest.'

'More restroom than rest,' I told him with a grin. 'They've drunk a lot of coffee.'

'They do seem a little...how you say? Grumpy?'

While communication between judges is expressly forbidden by the rules, that certainly wasn't a hardship for this group. Between competitors, Barbara sat with her head in her hands, obviously nursing a bad hangover.

Priscilla and her tech judge, whose face was as forgettable as his name, weren't so much as looking at each other. If they were trying to be discreet, it was having just the opposite effect. And if they'd had a lovers' quarrel, it must have been a humdinger.

'But you, Maggy?' Antonio said, standing up. 'You should be a TV persona. You have the audience captive.'

That certainly was true. The convention attendees seemed to be here for the duration. And who could blame them? If you had your choice between walking the exhibition floor or sitting and watching what was turning out to be a great competition, which would you choose?

'I believe you mean "captivated",' Marvin LaRoche said from behind me. 'For future reference.'

I rolled my eyes to let Antonio know LaRoche was an idiot and then turned to the man who would be coffee king. 'It's nearly three thirty, where have you been?'

'My apologies, Maggy,' he said, helping himself to a chocolate kiss undoubtedly meant for one of the specialty drinks. 'The reaction to my speech of last night was enormous. I just finished doing the last in a series of media interviews. It seems everyone wants to talk to me.'

Everyone *outside* the coffee community. Even Antonio, who had impeccable manners, was ignoring him now. I wondered how The Milkman had felt when his largest customer stood up on a podium and not only said he was going to buy his own dairies, but suggested everyone else do likewise.

Good thing LaRoche had Janalee and reporters or he'd be a mighty lonely man. Not that he'd notice.

'And the competition?' he was asking. 'I take it it's going well?'

'Perfectly, but then if the head judge had been there, the head judge would know that,' I said.

I knew I was being bitchy, but somehow I wanted to make him pay for being such a self-important jerk. If LaRoche was going to take the title of head judge, then he needed to fulfill the responsibilities. Even if I really hadn't wanted him there to horn in.

'You'll pardon me,' Antonio said, as petulance and self-interest duked it out in my head. 'I must make sure my people have taken care of everyone's needs.'

LaRoche waved him off like a housefly and turned to me. 'Now Maggy, I thought I explained—'

'Explained what? That your fifteen minutes of fame was more important than the competition?' Where I was getting *my* fifteen minutes of fame. 'The head judge is responsible for supervising the other six judges. If this was a sanctioned competition—'

LaRoche held up his hands. 'You're right, you're right—I surrender. I should have been here and I appreciate your leading the troops in my stead.'

Interesting that LaRoche reverted to military terms when attacked. Also interesting that even when he was apologizing, he could make me feel like a one-year-old. Even worse. At least Davy could pee on him.

Kate popped her head backstage. 'Jerome says it's time.'

Jerome apparently had Kate doing his errands. I was impressed.

'Be right there, thanks.' I turned back to LaRoche. 'Just to catch you up: the judges are doing fine. Two of them are sleeping together and one is hungover. The first-place trophy has boobs.'

I was walking as I was talking and LaRoche was scurrying after me.

'Oh, and your wife did a great job in her segment and is leading. Amy is with the next group. If one or both of them get into the finals, we'll have to talk about your recusing yourself.'

'Well, umm, I'm sure…'

'You'll find a seat next to the other judges.' As I stepped onstage and picked up my microphone, the crowd broke into applause.

God, I loved show business.

IF JANALEE WAS GOOD, Amy was stellar.

From the very start, she had the audience in the palm of her gauze-wrapped hand.

Maybe it was the rock music, a contrast to the jazz—smooth and otherwise—chosen by the other contestants. Or maybe it was her piercings, or her hair color, or her explosive specialty drink, complete with a depth charge in the bottom of the cup.

I prefer, though, to think it was her heart that won her the big points. Hand bandaged and covered by a plastic glove, she brewed and frothed, poured and presented with the best of them.

When the steam settled, Amy was standing onstage with Janalee and the rest of the finalists. 'And those are our six finalists,' I announced over the cheers of the crowd. 'We'll see them—and you—back here tomorrow at ten a.m. sharp for the finals. Good night, Java Ho!'

Another roar and I was offstage.

When I told the crowd good night, I wasn't kidding. It was nearly eight o'clock. Seven hours of barista competition and I was exhausted. And exhilarated. And starving.

'Bar?' Kate suggested in a rare moment of camaraderie.

'They have food there?'

'I think I saw some chips and salsa.'

'Sold.'

Jerome was coiling up the camera cable. 'Can I come?'

'We'd love to have you,' I said, 'but are you old enough?' Jerome looked twelve, but he acted thirty. It made judging his age tough.

'I'm twenty-one,' Jerome said.

Ahh, add the twelve and thirty, divide by two and you get twenty-one. I should be on TV.

'Why don't you two go on, and I'll be there in a minute,' I said.

I wanted to catch LaRoche before he left. I found him backstage, engaged in conversation with Antonio. LaRoche was waving a folder in Antonio's face. To The Milkman's credit, he was staying calm. If Antonio and his biceps wanted to, he could level LaRoche.

But to my astonishment, it was LaRoche who reached out and shoved Antonio. Antonio started toward him and I moved, intending to get between them. Just as I got there, though, The Milkman raised both hands in a sign of surrender—or maybe hands-off—and walked away.

'What was that all about?' I asked LaRoche.

'Not a thing,' he said, but his blue eyes looked moist.

He pulled out a handkerchief and blew his nose. 'Sorry, allergies. Now what can I do for you?'

I wasn't sure if I was buying the allergy story, but either way, it was none of my business. 'I wanted to talk to you about recusing yourself as judge tomorrow.'

'And why would I do that?' He tucked his hankie in his pocket.

'Because your wife and your star barista are finalists in the competition,' I said reasonably. 'I thought we had an understanding.'

'We had nothing of the sort. First of all, I'm the head judge.' He was holding up a finger to tick off points. At least that meant he'd be limited to ten. Unless he took his shoes off. 'The head judge doesn't vote.'

'Unless there's a tie.'

He ignored that and held up another finger. 'Second, Janalee is her own woman and to imply that she needs my help to win is a slap in the face to her.'

Obfuscation. I didn't bother to reply. We both knew he was using Janalee as a smoke screen to dodge the main question.

'And third.' He held up the appropriate finger. 'I understand Amy is going to work for you, so if *anyone* should recuse themselves, it's you.'

My mouth must have dropped open.

'There are secrets everywhere in this business, Maggy,' LaRoche continued, straightening his tie. 'The worst mistake you—or *anyone* else here can make—is to assume I don't know where they're buried.'

TWELVE

JUST WHAT DID LAROCHE KNOW?

Or think he knew?

I had to assume that Amy had told him she was leaving, despite the fact she and I hadn't talked details. Then again, maybe Caron or Sarah had blabbed, or maybe someone who overheard our conversation in the bar last night had snitched. Like the two old ladies.

I gave it more thought as I made my way to the bar. Besides LaRoche's insinuations, I was worried about Janalee and her reaction to Amy's leaving. And the gossip, of course. News travels like wildfire at conventions. And while we were on the subject of fires, people wouldn't really believe I set the one at Janalee's in order to steal Amy, would they?

It was ridiculous, but since when...

'Maggy! We're here.' Kate and Jerome were waving me over.

'Don't worry,' Kate said as I joined them at the bar. 'Jack's legal. The bartender checked his ID.'

'No judge of age apparently,' I said, shooting a smile at Jerome.

The bartender—the same one who had waited on us the night before—came over. 'Pinot Noir?'

'Good memory,' I said. 'But I think I need something stronger.'

'Cabernet?'

'Perfect.' I slid on to the barstool next to Kate.

'Much as I hate to admit it,' she said, 'you did a spectacular job today.'

'Thanks.' The bartender slid over my glass and I took a slug. 'You're not going to edit me out of the finished program, are you?'

Kate blushed under the freckles. 'To be honest, I had every intention of leaving you on the cutting-room floor.'

Jerome leaned forward so he could see past Kate to me. 'Why?'

'I ruined her on-camera career,' I said mildly.

'You overestimate yourself,' Kate said, gesturing for a menu. 'If I had wanted a career in TV, I would have stayed in TV.'

'I'll have a 7UP,' Jerome said to the bartender before turning to us. 'So why were you going to cut her out of the show?' he asked curiously.

Kate looked up from her perusal of the menu. 'To torture her.' She held up the menu to the bartender. 'Can we have an order of nachos, pizza bread and some pot stickers?'

'Slumming, Kate?' I asked mildly.

She shrugged. 'I didn't see bruschetta on the menu.'

The bartender looked at me. 'With that varied menu, sure you don't want a beer?'

'True,' I said. 'It is the universal donor of beverages.'

Jerome laughed at that. 'A blood type joke—I like it.'

Yet more proof the kid had medical problems, either now or in the past. Or he hung around blood banks. I opened my mouth to ask, but Kate interrupted.

'So, rumor has it you burned down LaRoche's place.'

'Where in the world did you hear that?' I demanded.

'How else do you explain getting to the scene of the fire so fast?'

'Who said I was there?' I was hoping the woman was just fishing for information.

'The police scanner.' Kate stirred her Diet Pepsi and house brand.

Great. The police were talking about me over the radio. Why? Because I was a suspect, or because I was the sheriff's girlfriend?

Which brought up an interesting dilemma: did I admit to Kate that I was with Pavlik when the call came in? It would answer her question. It would also open us up to whatever speculation that caused.

I decided to stonewall for now. 'I saw the fire trucks on my way home,' I fibbed. 'I just followed them.'

'Your way home from—'

'What fire are we talking about?' Jerome asked.

'Janalee's Place.' Grateful for the interruption, I explained.

'They're sure it was arson?' Jerome asked when I was done.

'That's what my sources tell me,' Kate interjected mysteriously. Since both Janalee and LaRoche were talking openly about the arson, Kate's source was probably as mysterious as this morning's paper.

I said as much.

Kate sniffed. 'Don't be ridiculous. This came from the horse's mouth—*your* horse's mouth.' She looked expectantly at me.

'Who?' I asked, cautious.

'Your squeeze,' she tried.

When I still didn't bite, she rolled her eyes. 'Stop playing stupid. I mean the sheriff, you idiot.'

Oh. Him.

AFTER DRINKS, I RETURNED to the competition room. I'd been so upset after my encounter with LaRoche earlier, that I'd forgotten to check on the trophies in preparation for tomorrow's finals. I could do it in the morning, but this way I didn't have to arrive so early.

And I needed to get a good night's sleep tonight. I'd let Kate get to me and probably had a glass or two more wine than I really needed.

I wondered what Pavlik had told her. I assumed that it was merely that the fire was arson. I was certain he wouldn't say anything implicating me. I also couldn't imagine him saying something about our being together.

If he had, Kate would have been blabbing about that, too. And there was nothing I could do about it.

I turned my attention to the trophies. I could make them, at least, bend to my will. The awards were grouped in the middle of the table so I spaced them out, leaving the first-place trophy in the center. Then, pulling down a corner of the tablecloth that was flipped up, I surveyed the scene.

I still wasn't happy with the first-place trophy, which Sarah had promptly dubbed 'Slut in a cup' after today's unveiling. There was nothing I could do about that either, though. And the five runner-up trophies were just fine. I checked my watch—nearly twelve fifteen. T-minus nine hours, forty-five minutes. Time to go home.

I wasn't staying nights at the convention hotel, since home was so close by. Besides, Frank needed me and, honestly, there were some nights I needed Frank.

This was one of them.

I also could have used a little Pavlik, even if I was unhappy he'd found time to tell the town crier about the arson. And not tell his…whatever I was.

But a girl always has her dog, thank God. When I got home, I flopped down on the couch and snuggled my toes into Frank's thick fur. Then I looked at the phone. Should I call Pavlik and just ask him about Kate? Tell him what people were saying?

Probably not. My experience with authority—legal authority—was that what seems common knowledge may not be. Just because people were gossiping, didn't mean that Pavlik knew it.

So why would I tell him and possibly implicate myself?

Because there was a part of me that wanted Pavlik to assure me everything was OK, of course. That daddy—or husband, or boyfriend—would take care of me. But I'd found out when Ted left me that the person best suited to taking care of me was me.

In just a few hours, I needed to preside over the finals of the barista competition and the awarding of the trophies. I had to get through that before I did anything else.…

I leaned down and gave Frank a good scratch behind the ear. 'Tomorrow, Frank. I'll give Pavlik a call tomorrow after the competition. But not to tell him what I know, but to find out what *he* knows.'

THIRTEEN

TOMORROW WAS, as Scarlett O'Hara said, another day. It just wasn't the day I expected.

Saturday dawned bright and early. But then what day doesn't? Sure, some dawns are brighter than others, but they're all lighter than the night.

Or are they?

Because here I was, standing over the body of Marvin LaRoche. Murder weapon in one hand, blood on the other.

'Call 911,' I said.

FOURTEEN

ON TV, THE FIRST COP to arrive on the scene would be the handsome love interest, Pavlik.

But this was cable access, so what we got were rent-a-cops from the convention center. There were three of them. One was fat, one was skinny and one was just right.

'Can't you get her to stop that?' the big rent-a-cop asked, hitching up his pants.

'What?' Sarah asked, looking over her shoulder at Janalee. 'The screaming or the crying?'

'I'd take either,' the cop muttered and walked away to talk on his giant walkie-talkie.

'Would it be against type for him to be talking on a little flip-phone?' I asked Sarah.

I was very busy thinking about all things inconsequential. Which was pretty much everything except Marvin LaRoche's body. *That* didn't bear thinking about.

'Probably,' she said. 'Image is everything when you're a rent-a-cop.'

'I suppose.' We were sitting on two of the judges' chairs, waiting for the authorities. I looked down at my hand. 'I really, *really* want to wash the blood off.'

'Don't blame you. Looks like it's going bad.'

Sarah was right. The blood was turning brown. Crusty brown with red and white flecks. Yuck. 'I think I'm going to be sick. Is that white gunk brain matter?'

Sarah leaned in a little closer. 'Nah. Look, it's fuzzy. Like it's growing something.'

I couldn't look. I was afraid I was going to get sick. 'Aren't the CSI people supposed to be here? Taking samples with cotton swabs and squeeze bottles? And then letting me frickin' wash?'

'Only on TV,' Sarah said, taking a puff on her nicotine inhaler. 'I have a friend whose husband disappeared. I guess the guy's body was found in Idaho a week later, but she didn't find out for nearly a year.'

That didn't seem right. 'But what about DNA and databases and all?' I asked, happy to be distracted from whatever was growing on the Petri dish that used to be my hand.

'Like I said, that's just on TV. She said they can't do DNA for everybody because crime labs are underfunded. And even when they do, it takes a long time to get results because there's a backlog because they're also understaffed.'

'That's awful.' I looked down at my hand. 'I think I'm going to throw up.'

'Concentrate on something else.'

'Like what? The body on the floor? The fact it's LaRoche, my arch-enemy, who accused me of stealing his barista last night? Or maybe that I touched the murder weapon and now have the victim's blood on my hand?'

'Last night? What happened last night?' Sarah asked, choosing to ignore the rest of my ramblings.

'I had an argument with LaRoche.'

Sarah looked heavenward, but I continued. 'Listen, his barista and his wife were finalists, and he was head judge. The right thing to do was recuse himself. I was just trying to get him to see the light.'

'So you won.' Sarah cocked her head toward the body. 'LaRoche not only saw the light, he went *toward* the light.'

Any other time I would have laughed at that. Drying blood on your hand and a dead man on your stage impairs your sense of humor. I watched as the EMTs finally arrived. They were hurrying, but not save-a-life hurrying. More like make-sure-he's-dead hurrying.

'So did anyone else hear the argument?' Sarah asked.

'No, thank God. No one was there to hear.'

'Not last night, at least.' Sarah stuck her puffer back in her pocket.

'What do you mean?' I looked around.

Kate and Jerome were busy following the EMTs with the camera. Jill still had her lens trained on the body, and the audience and judges had been herded to the far side of the hall. Amy, Janalee and Davy were sitting quietly in the corner with the other contestants.

'There's nobody to hear me,' I said.

'You do know you have your mic on, right?'

A Lavaliere microphone was pinned to my sweater. I thought it would be easier than using the hand-held for the finals. Was it truly on? Had everyone heard what I was saying?

Trying to seem nonchalant, I glanced toward the knot of people on the other side of the room. Henry and Sophie waved back. Oh, God.

I jumped up and went to pull off the microphone. 'My bloody hand—I can't touch the microphone,' I whispered urgently to Sarah. 'You have to get it off.'

'You sound like something out of a British horror movie,' she said, snickering. She grasped the wrist of one of her hands with the other, like she was trying to keeping it from attacking. 'My hand, my bloody hand—get it off, get it off!'

'Will you shut up?' I hissed. 'This isn't funny.'

Sarah just cocked her head.

No help apparently forthcoming from her, I managed to pull the clip-on microphone off with my left hand. I was still tangled in the wire that ran inside my sweater to the pack positioned at the back of my waist.

'The on/off switch is on the pack,' I said. 'Can you reach it?' I was trying to get at it with my left arm, but it didn't seem to bend that way.

'Can I help?' a familiar voice said.

I hadn't noticed the cavalry—in the form of a cadre of sheriff's deputies—arrive, but I sure was happy to see them. And the sheriff, himself.

I turned to Pavlik. 'I'm so glad you're here. Can you turn this microphone off?'

Pavlik looked quizzically at me, but he checked the pack. 'It *is* off.'

I threw Sarah a dirty look, and she grinned. 'Got your mind off throwing up, didn't I?'

I was at a loss for words. The thought that Sarah had been torturing me in order to be kind was staggering. And a little sick.

Pavlik nodded toward my hand. 'Blood?'

'It isn't my blood,' I said, though at this point I kind of wished it was. Your own blood was bad enough, but somebody else's blood drying on your hand? That was downright creepy.

'There was blood on the tablecloth, and I accidentally put my hand in it,' I explained in a rush. 'The little rent-a-cop said I couldn't wash it. Which I knew, of course, from TV, but I was getting a little crazy, what with the blood getting—' I looked down at my hand— 'crusty and all.' I gagged.

Pavlik took my arm and sat me back down. 'Before you fall down.' He waved a deputy over. 'Can you ask the crime scene guys if they need to take a sample of this blood?'

If?

Of course they were going to take a sample. How else could the police mistakenly send me to prison, where I would be Big Bertha's girlfriend until I was finally freed by a criminal justice class some twenty years later?

I was the star of my very own made-for-TV movie.

Pavlik knelt down in front of me. 'They're probably going to take a sample, just to confirm it's the same as on the tablecloth and the trophy.'

'There *was* no blood on the trophy,' I said. 'And I should know. After all, I was the one caught brandishing it over the body, just like in the movies.'

'From what I hear,' Pavlik said, 'two hundred people saw you pick it up.'

'Maybe she picked it up to cover the fact her finger-prints were already on it,' Sarah said helpfully.

'I'm not that smart,' I growled.

'There is that.' Sarah was mulling it over.

'The killer tried to wipe off the trophy.' Pavlik apparently had decided to move the conversation along. 'But the felt fabric on the bottom caught quite a bit of blood.'

I nodded. I was holding my hand out to the side, trying to keep it beyond my peripheral vision.

'They'll need your fingerprints, too,' he continued.

'To eliminate me?' I squeaked.

'Sure,' Pavlik said, sounding preoccupied. He'd stood up and was looking over at the trophy. 'Just what is that supposed to be?'

'What does it look like?' Sarah asked before I could answer.

'A big-breasted woman in a hot tub?' Pavlik hazarded.

'Close,' I said dryly. 'A barista in a coffee cup.'

'OK, I can see that.' Pavlik squinted. 'And the two…' He cupped his hands.

'Headlights,' Sarah supplied.

'Right,' Pavlik said. 'They'll likely fit the indentations on LaRoche's forehead.' He pointed toward the body.

I cleared my throat. 'Listen, are those crime scene guys going to be coming soon?' I asked, holding up my hand.

'Yup. Sorry.' Pavlik waved over a man with a tool-box.

'You're looking a little green,' Sarah said as she moved aside to let the guy in.

'She'll be fine.' Pavlik crouched back down in front of me. 'Just let Jim here—' he gestured to the tech— 'take a sample and fingerprint you.'

'And then can I wash my hand?' I asked.

'Yes, then you can wash your hand,' Pavlik said gently. 'Now I need to talk to the rest of the people here.'

As Pavlik stood up, I grabbed his arm. With the clean hand. 'Listen, someone may tell you that Amy—she was the manager of Janalee's Place, you'll remember—is coming to work for Caron and me, and that's true.'

'OK.' He started to move away.

I tightened my grip. 'They also may tell you that I burned down Janalee's Place.'

Pavlik's jaw dropped.

'But that's *not* true,' I added hastily.

'Good,' he said, looking a trifle dazed. 'That's good.' And he walked away.

SWABBED, FINGERPRINTED and washed, I went into the exhibit hall in search of a friendly face, preferably one that wasn't actively gossiping about me.

'Maybe I'm being paranoid,' I said to Kate, who also had been tossed out of the crime scene. We were walking down the main aisle of the exhibit hall. 'I feel like everyone is looking and whispering.'

'No, I don't think so,' she said. 'Did you know they confiscated our tape?'

'What do you mean?'

'I mean they made Jack give them his cassette.'

'No,' I protested. 'What I wanted to know was whether you meant "No, you don't think I'm being paranoid," or "No, you don't think people are looking and whispering".'

'Oh, they're looking and whispering, all right,' Kate confirmed.

Great.

'Anyway,' Kate continued, 'I thought the kid was going to chain himself to the tapes. He was arguing with the police and citing the First Amendment when I left.'

You had to wonder why a college student was more concerned about freedom of the press than the press, herself.

'Good for Jerome,' I said. 'At least *he* has the courage to stand up for what he believes.'

'Yes, yes, yes,' Kate said, rolling her eyes. 'But let's get back to you and the whispering and the pointing. Rumor has it you burned down Janalee's to steal Amy and that LaRoche knew it.'

Kate was trying to get a rise out of me again for her newspaper, and I had no intention of confirming or denying what Marvin LaRoche had said to me. I didn't spend all those years in public relations for nothing.

'Why would you say that?' I said evenly. '*If* LaRoche or anyone else thought I had something to do with the fire, they're mistaken.'

As I spoke, Kate was fishing through her voluminous handbag. I heard a muffled 'click' and then a whirr.

A tape recorder—I couldn't believe it, even of Kate.

'You're trying to tape me,' I said. 'After all we've been through together the last few days. How could you? We're partners.'

She pulled the tape recorder out of her bag. 'Partners? We have a seventy–thirty split, your favor. *And* you're the star. You consider that partners?'

Worked for me. 'Seventy percent of nothing is nothing,' I pointed out. 'We have no profits and no program.'

'Only because you killed the chief judge.'

'I did *not* kill LaRoche,' I said, perhaps too vehemently. The exhibit hall went silent. Now people definitely were staring.

'Arson and murder.' Kate smiled blissfully. 'If you thought there was speculation before, just you wait.'

'Kate.' Jerome came up to us before I could answer. Or slap her silly. 'I'm glad I found you. I'm concerned about our footage. Maybe if you spoke to the police—'

'Not now, Jack,' Kate said. 'I have more important fish to fry.' She threw me a dirty grin and walked away.

'What could be more important than the First Amendment?' Jerome asked me, looking shocked.

'The Eighth, perhaps?' I muttered, watching Kate stop to talk to a group of people. They all looked our way. 'Cruel and unusual punishment.'

He gave me a knowing grin. 'Don't worry, I've dealt with worse.'

I'd been thinking about Kate torturing me—guess I wasn't the only one. While a case could be made that I was capable of taking care of myself, picking on Jerome was like teasing a puppy. A very smart, bespectacled, Mr Peabody-like puppy.

'Listen,' I said, linking arms with him. 'I assume you have some time on your hands now. Want to help me?'

'I'd be honored,' he said, looking pleased.

'Great. You and Jill have been going around taping people—sort of the sights and sounds of Java Ho, right?'

I had two reasons for asking the question. First, something they had inadvertently captured on tape might suggest who had wanted LaRoche dead. Second, I wanted to make sure they hadn't caught *me* on tape, sounding like I wanted LaRoche dead.

'Correct,' he said, turning to me. 'For B-roll.'

The term B-roll is a throwback to when film was edited from reels or rolls. Editors would use B-roll, or secondary footage on another reel, to provide segues and context between segments of the main event: the A-roll.

'But since the police took everything we shot this morning,' he went on, 'I guess B becomes A, doesn't it?'

'Or, since there is no barista competition,' I countered, 'it's all B-roll. Garbage.'

'Never garbage,' Jerome said, aghast at the thought. 'Tape and film—they are what we chronicle our lives and our times on. What would we know about the 1940s or '50s or '60s without TV or movies?'

'Well, some of us actually remember a few of those years,' I pointed out.

'I'm sorry, I didn't mean to…I mean, you look so young.'

Yeah, right. I waved him off. 'I know, I know, to someone your age, *Raiders of the Lost Ark* is a classic. Me, I'm more *Rear Window* or *North by Northwest*.'

'Quite honestly, I love old movies,' Jerome said. 'It's one of the reasons I decided to study Communication and Theatre Arts.'

Interesting kid, this one. 'I'm afraid I'm a bit of a movie junkie myself,' I admitted.

'My father says that we're all addicted to something,' Jerome said. 'The trick is to make sure it's something that's good for us.'

Just then I caught a glimpse of Sarah heading out of the door of the exhibit hall. 'Listen,' I said to Jerome, 'I need to do a few things first, but how can I get a look at those tapes?'

'The editing suite at the school would probably be easiest,' Jerome said. 'There's a lot of footage, and we can get through it faster there.'

'Perfect.' I checked my watch. Could it only be one thirty? 'Want to meet there at say, three?'

'I'll be there.' Jerome gave me directions and then hesitated.

'Something wrong?' I asked.

He cocked his head. 'I'm just wondering when you're going to tell me what you're doing. As you said, there's no hope in salvaging the show.'

What did I say to him? I'm afraid my boyfriend is going to arrest me for murdering my competitor, burning down his shop and stealing his barista?

Jerome would think I was a lunatic. But the truth was, that's exactly what I was afraid of.

'I'm afraid my boyfriend is going to arrest me for murdering my competitor, burning down his shop and stealing his barista.'

I braced myself, waiting for Jerome's reaction. Surprise, reassurance, commitment—probably of me, to an insane asylum.

But he just nodded. 'Makes sense. See you at three.'

Yeah, see you at three.

FIFTEEN

I FOUND SARAH WITH the smokers outside the revolving door. I was reminded of Jerome's dad and his thoughts on addiction.

'Maybe you should take up red wine,' I said. 'At least there are health benefits to that.'

'I'm not smoking,' Sarah protested. She was standing next to a red-haired woman with permanently-pursed lips and nicotine-stained hands. When the woman exhaled, Sarah centered herself in the cloud of smoke and breathed deeply. 'Oh, God, that's so good,' she said, as Red looked at her uneasily.

I pulled Sarah away. 'Have you lost your mind? You're exchanging air with that woman. Her germs, her breath, her smoke. In some cultures you'd have to marry her.'

Sarah waved me off. 'I've had a bad day. You were there. We found Marvin LaRoche dead. I'll breathe anybody's air I want to.'

I have to admit I hadn't given much thought to Sarah's reaction to the death of LaRoche, a longtime client. Questionable tactics aside, Sarah had tried to help me in the competition room. The least I could do was offer her a shoulder.

'I'm sorry, Sarah,' I said, patting her arm. 'You knew LaRoche better than I did. How are you doing?'

My friend looked surprised that I was being so solicitous. 'Why…why, thanks for asking Maggy. I do feel a little light-headed.' She put a hand to her head. 'Perhaps a cigarette might get me past the worst of it.'

'Shame on you,' I scolded her. 'At least I'm honest enough to admit I didn't like LaRoche—'

Janalee LaRoche chose that moment to rotate out of the revolving door, though 'chose' wasn't the right word. Janalee didn't look like she was capable of making any decisions, including walking and talking.

I touched her shoulder, the one without Davy on it, praying that she hadn't heard me. 'Janalee, I'm so sorry. Is there anything I can do?'

Janalee had a cloth diaper draped over the baby's face and all I could see of him was a pair of eyes. Apparently she was trying to shield him from the smoke, though the widening wet spot on Davy's bottom argued that the diaper might be better employed on that end.

Janalee waved me over to an area that was relatively smoke-free. Sarah didn't follow us. Instead, she edged closer to the redhead, who, in turn, edged away. Any minute now they'd be in the bushes.

'I can't believe this is all happening.' Janalee took a deep breath. 'First the fire and now Marvin? It's just too much, and with Amy leaving, too…' Tears started to flow.

'I'm so sorry about that,' I said, tears welling up in my eyes, too. 'Why don't you just keep Amy?' Caron was going to kill me.

But Janalee just smiled sadly. 'You're sweet, Maggy, but Amy's not my property. We'll have to let her decide what she wants to do.'

I guess we did, dammit. And now that LaRoche was gone, I wondered whether she would, indeed, stay with Janalee.

'But there *is* something you can do for me,' Janalee was saying as she patted Davy on his wet butt.

'Of course, anything,' I said, hoping she didn't want me to change him. Or babysit.

'Take over Java Ho in Marvin's stead.'

Even worse.

'But don't you think we should cancel the rest of the convention?'

After all, Sunday was always the slowest day at a convention. People getting ready to leave and all. The exhibit hall would be open, of course, and there was a frothing clinic and a cupping—the coffee equivalent of a wine-tasting. Neither would pull in the kind of numbers...

Janalee was patting my hand now, instead of Davy's wet bum. 'It was Marvin's dream, and he would want us to see it through. Would you do that for him?' Her blue eyes were overflowing again.

No, I wouldn't do it for him. But I'd do it for Janalee, with her soggy eyes and her equally soggy baby. Especially if it would make her stop touching me with her soggy hand. 'Sure, I'll do it.'

'Thank you.' Removing the diaper from Davy's head, she reached in and pulled a folder out of the sling. Mercifully, it was dry. 'Here's the information you'll need. The banquet is tonight.'

'Banquet?'

'Don't worry. Cocktails at six thirty, dinner at seven thirty, and everything is set with the caterers. Your contact with them is named Penny and she's a marvel. Now Marvin was supposed to speak, but I've asked Levitt Fredericks of EarthBean to take his place.'

Not a bad idea. EarthBean's agenda would have equal time to LaRoche's.

'And one more favor, Maggy?'

This time I didn't say 'anything'. 'What is it?'

She played her hands through Davy's downy hair, focusing on him. 'I know I should come and say something about Marvin, but I just can't.' She looked up at me. 'Would you? Would you tell people what kind of man he was? I'm afraid they will just remember his rant in the keynote speech. Marvin wasn't like that.'

The hell he wasn't. But those eyes were pumping water again. 'Tell you what, Janalee. I think it would be much more appropriate for Sarah Kingston to do it, instead of me. She's known LaRo...Marvin, so much longer.' And she, at least, was unlikely to become a suspect in his murder. 'Why don't I ask her?'

Janalee clapped in joy, nearly catching Davy upside the head. 'Wonderful idea, Maggy. Marvin had great respect for Sarah.'

Everyone had great respect for Sarah. Or else.

'Perfect. Then it's settled,' I said, happy to see that Sarah was still sucking smoke to my right. I wouldn't have to track her down. 'Now you go home and rest.'

'I will,' she promised and started down the sidewalk. Then she turned back. 'And Maggy, just so you know. No matter what people may say, I know you didn't have anything to do with either the fire or Marvin's death.'

PULLING SARAH TO the side, I broke the news.

'Me? Speak? What am I going to say?'

'Please, like you haven't spoken at a million events.'

'Real estate events,' she clarified. 'Most everyone is either talking or dead drunk.'

As opposed to our convention, where they were just dead.

'You're not getting out of this,' I said sternly. 'You will do five minutes on Marvin LaRoche. You will be nice, but not too nice, or people will storm the stage. They won't have forgotten his speech from Thursday night.'

'Don't worry,' Sarah said, 'people never badmouth the dead.'

'Only because it's not as much fun as badmouthing the living,' I said. 'I can't believe we're going ahead with this thing.'

'You're telling me,' Sarah said. 'I wasn't even planning on going to the banquet. What am I supposed to wear?'

I took a sniff. 'Something that doesn't smell like smoked fish. You didn't stink this bad when you were smoking.'

Sarah twisted her head toward her shoulder and got a whiff. 'Whew, she smokes some cheap-ass cigarettes, I tell you.'

'I don't think huffers can be choosers,' I said. 'Listen, I'll meet you in the Crystal Ballroom at six. Cocktails are at six thirty, dinner seven thirty, and I'll start the program the minute the first person sets down his or her fork.'

I got out my car keys. 'Believe me, tonight is going to be short and sweet.'

It turned out to be neither.

WHEN I ARRIVED AT Brookhills Community College, it was three on the dot.

BCC is a two-year college that feeds into the four-year university system. Most of the kids who go there are local, often living at home.

Eric had considered attending BCC his first two years, before transferring to a bigger school out of state. I had encouraged him to go away to school. After all, living away from home is an important developmental step.

Besides, much as I love my son, I had imagined an adult lifestyle: romantic dinners for Ted and me, without first having to clear dirty socks off the dining room table. Nights at the theater, without being summoned away during intermission by a panicky text message. Drinks on the way home from work, without worrying about cooking dinner.

Now I could do all of those things. Only, alone. Moral: be careful what you wish for.

Jerome met me at the main door of the arts building and led me to the editing suite. 'I've got everything all set,' he said as he waved me to a chair at the console. 'I just didn't know where you wanted to start.'

He settled into the chair next to me. A picture of La-Roche at the lectern was frozen on the screen in front of us. 'First thing we taped was Marvin's speech. We only had one camera, as you'll remember, so I can't give you any crowd reaction.'

Crowd reaction would have been nice. Perhaps some-one screaming, 'I'm going to kill you, LaRoche'—now *that* would have been perfect.

'How about after the speech?' I asked. 'Did you get crowd shots then?'

'Of course.' Jerome spun a dial and the tape fast-forwarded. LaRoche's speech was a lot more enjoyable condensed to five seconds and without sound. Jerome slowed the image to real time as LaRoche stepped off the stage. 'I think I got him talking to a few people here, shaking hands.'

The tape showed LaRoche approaching the first row of attendees to glad-hand them. The pained expressions on the shakees' faces spoke volumes about both La-Roche's hearty grip and their feelings for him.

A blonde woman who was dragooned into shaking hands looked around, apparently wary of being seen consorting with the enemy. It was the visibly irate man behind her who caught my eye, though. Levitt Freder-icks. He seemed to be speaking to someone next to him, but he was glaring at LaRoche.

'Can you get any sound on this?'

'I can, but it's mostly "Born in the USA".' Jerome turned on the audio.

He was right, I couldn't hear anything above the music except for the general murmur of the crowd. 'Can't you take the music out? Separate the tracks or something?'

'Maybe the FBI facility in Quantico could do that,' he said apologetically, 'but I'm afraid this is the best I can do in a community college.'

Dang. Why isn't anything the way it is in the movies?

'But I do think I have more footage with that tall gray-haired man in it, if that's what you're looking for.'

That was exactly what I was looking for. 'He's not with LaRoche, by any chance, is he?' And perhaps has a bloody trophy in his hand?

'In fact, he *is* with Marvin.' Jerome spun the dial. 'Last night. Friday.'

Bingo. We had found the body this morning—had it just been this morning?—and today was Saturday. That meant LaRoche died sometime between eight p.m. last night, when he and I had our little dust-up, and a little bit before ten this morning when Sarah and I discovered the body.

So when was he killed—late last night or early this morning? Maybe his clothes would tell me.

I thought of LaRoche lying there, eyes staring out from under his bloody forehead. But what had he been wearing? A suit, of course. A dark one. But since he always wore dark suits that wouldn't help me much. What else?

Some people are born observers. And rememberers. Me? I'm a natural forgetter. I can't remember what I was wearing yesterday, much less anyone else. I introduced and re-introduced myself to people I'd already met.

Still, shouldn't I remember what the dead body I'd stumbled across this morning looked like? Most people would see it in their dreams. Or their nightmares.

Jerome had found the right place on the tape. 'I was shooting the exhibitors closing down their booths for the evening. It seemed like it would make good B-roll.'

The exhibit hall closed to the public at eight p.m. and not a moment earlier, with Sarah at the helm. That meant the tape was shot *after* I'd seen LaRoche just before eight.

The monitor showed a vendor smoothing a giant dust cover over a counter filled with espresso machines. As he did, LaRoche walked into the picture on one side and then out the other. He was wearing his signature dark suit, but I couldn't see either the shirt or the tie as Jerome's camera swiveled to follow.

I tried to figure out which way the camera was pointing. Since most of the exhibitors already were shut down, I couldn't find a landmark. 'Do you remember what direction he was going?'

Jerome froze the image and sat back in his swivel chair. 'Let's see. I was in the center aisle and this was L'Café's booth. I know that because I had the guy sign a release.'

'Good.' I leaned forward to get a better look at the screen. 'The center aisle runs north and south, so La-Roche is either going north, towards the competition room, or south toward the Grand Foyer and the front door.' Please God, let it be north.

'North.'

Yes!

Jerome pointed. 'See the restroom signs? They're on the back wall of the exhibit hall.'

'The north wall.' How could I have missed that? Others may scope out the emergency exits when they enter a building. Me? I always know where the restrooms are.

Jerome started the tape moving again. As LaRoche got closer to the restrooms, a man stepped out of a side aisle and stopped him. It was Levitt Fredericks.

'I suppose we're too far away to hear anything,' I said tentatively, not wanting to ask another—or perhaps the same—stupid question.

'Yup.' Jerome turned toward me and gave me a big grin. 'Until they start yelling.'

'They yell?'

'They yell.'

He turned up the volume. Generic convention noises, and then: '…not my problem. My responsibility is to my customers and, when we go public, to my shareholders,' LaRoche was saying.

Levitt grabbed his arm. 'What about the world, the environment?' he asked. 'The families in Mexico and Central America? The men, women and children who harvest the beans, allowing you to reap the profits. Do they mean nothing to you? These people are living in poverty.'

LaRoche shook him off and as he did, I caught sight of his tie. Burgundy. And the shirt was white. 'I *am* concerned about families,' LaRoche said. '*My* family, first and foremost.'

'So that's your only concern. *Your* family.'

'Yes, however you want to define it.' For the first time, LaRoche looked truly angry. 'If more people took care of their own flesh and blood, we wouldn't need groups like yours handing out charity.'

'You, sir, are well aware that EarthBean doesn't supply handouts,' Levitt said as LaRoche walked away from
him, nearly colliding with a dark-haired man trying to
get around them.

Levitt dodged after LaRoche and continued: 'We provide tools for the poor to help themselves...' The rest
was lost as the two turned the corner, either to the men's
room or, beyond that, the entrance to the competition
room.

Jerome sat back again in his chair and steepled his
fingers. 'Not bad, huh?'

Not bad? It was all a girl wanting to divert suspi-
cion away from herself could ask for. 'I could kiss you,
Jerome,' I said. 'But I won't,' I added hastily, 'lest people
talk.'

Jerome looked skyward and spread his hands in a
helpless gesture. 'Just my luck.'

'Yeah, right.' I looked at the clock on the console. It
was almost four. I had to meet Sarah at six and, now
that I was feeling better, I wanted to make a stop on my
way home. 'I probably should run, but is there anything
else I should see?'

'That's the last of what I taped yesterday, and I went
through the footage of the barista competition. Marvin
was sitting next to the judges the whole time. Then this
morning...'

He let it trail off. This morning, of course, Marvin
LaRoche wasn't sitting anywhere.

I wondered what we should do with the tape. I could
take it along and give it to Pavlik, but wouldn't that break
some kind of chain of evidence? No, better to keep it in
Jerome's possession.

'Take good care of that tape,' I said as I stood up. 'The police are going to come looking for it.'

He was puzzled. 'How do you know that?'

'Because I'm going to tell them to.' I smiled. 'So you'll be at the banquet, right?'

'Well, I was going to ask Kate that before she took off so abruptly. Do you still want us to cover it, despite the fact the barista competition is—' he spread his hands out wide— 'no more?'

Good question. But I liked having Jerome and his camera around. Sort of a videotape safety net. 'Sure,' I said. 'Maybe you can turn this into something useful. A class project of some kind.'

Jerome stood up to escort me to the door. He was thinking. 'Interesting idea. Not a feature film, of course, but maybe a short. Or a documentary.'

'After all, how many college students are ever involved in a homicide investigation? And who knows, maybe you can enter it in a film festival or something.'

I left Jerome with visions of documentaries Sundancing in his head.

Me, I was thinking of burgundy ties.

Specifically, LaRoche's burgundy tie flipped over his shoulder as he lay dead.

Some things you just don't forget. At least not for long.

SIXTEEN

THERE'S NOTHING LIKE narrowing down a time of death and finding an alternative murder suspect to raise a woman's spirits.

Not that I wished Levitt ill, but it was pretty clear from the tape that he had an argument with LaRoche after my argument. And the burgundy tie proved that LaRoche had been killed in the same clothes he had been wearing Friday. That meant he was killed Friday night, not Saturday morning. That was Friday night— after his argument with Levitt.

In my relief and haste, I hadn't noticed if there was a time stamp on the tape that would prove exactly when it was recorded and cement my alibi. I'd met Kate and Jerome for drinks after seeing LaRoche, so the timeline seemed pretty clear. First my fight, then Levitt's.

So why was LaRoche going back to the competition room when he had encountered Levitt? Or wasn't he? Maybe I was jumping to conclusions and LaRoche was simply aiming for the men's room. Life would have been so much simpler for me if he had been found dead under the urinal, instead of the trophy table. Chances were pretty good I wouldn't have found him there.

But no. LaRoche had ended up in the competition room. Why? I didn't have an answer to that one yet. But I did have a banquet to run.

On the way home, my minivan made a stop at my favorite dress shop. Or what used to be my favorite dress shop. Since my divorce, money and the occasion to wear a nice dress had definitely been limited.

Still, I'd missed Bruce Paul Goodman—both the store and the person. BPG was Brookhills' premier women's clothing store. Bruce carried more than designer dresses, of course. He had designer handbags and sweaters and shoes—oh, my! He even had a designer dog named Toto.

Bruce greeted me when I stepped in the door.

'Maggy,' he said, giving me a hug, 'it's been far too long.'

'You're telling me,' I said, gazing around. 'And how I've missed you all: you and Nicole, and Vera and Kate.'

'And me and Toto, too?' Jacqueline, my favorite sales-woman called from the dressing area.

'*That* goes without saying.' I gave her a wave, Toto an ear-scratch, and looked around.

Pre-divorce, a trip to Bruce's would have been an all-afternoon affair. Me, trapped in the dressing room, and Bruce and Jacqueline bringing armload after armload of fabulous clothes I 'just had to see'.

I know, I had been badmouthing Caron's designer-barista aspirations, and here *I* was lusting after the tex-tile equivalent. Luckily, post-divorce poverty had pretty much broken me of that habit.

'I should never have walked in the door,' I moaned, shaking my head at the racks laden with beautiful things. 'I have about ten minutes to find a dress that I can afford.' I held up a finger. 'Key word, Bruce: *afford*.'

He looked taken aback. 'Ten minutes? To shop?'

Jacqueline, who was already picking through the racks, just turned and stared, a Nicole Miller hanging off her arm.

'I know,' I said, ruefully. 'The concept boggles the mind. I should probably go.' I started to leave before they had a chance to stop me.

Then I saw a dress. Sleek black, with a high neck and long sleeves. It looked unassuming—except for the cut-outs that bared each shoulder.

Bruce saw me pause. 'It's your size,' he said.

He just didn't play fair.

THE WORLD WAS conspiring against my meeting Sarah on time.

First, the stop at Bruce Paul's—admittedly, my own fault. On the way home, I encountered an unexpected traffic jam on Brookhill Road. Likely a soccer game at the high school or a dance recital at Tiny Tots.

Then, when I arrived home, I found Pavlik waiting in the driveway.

Now this was what I call a 'good problem'. Good, because he looked exceptionally handsome and because I wanted to pry some information from him. And a problem, because I was too short on time to take full advantage in either of these ways.

I gave Pavlik a quick kiss and resisted snuggling deep into his buttery leather jacket. It took me about three seconds to decide not to chastise him for telling Kate about the arson and not telling me.

'Listen, I'm a little pressed for time,' I said, smiling apologetically up into his face. Pavlik was a good six inches taller than me, so I spent a lot of time looking up at him, though not necessarily at the angle I wanted to.

'Janalee asked me to take over the banquet,' I continued, 'and that means I have to be dressed and out of here in less than an hour.'

'Not a problem,' Pavlik said. 'I just wanted to stop by and see how you are.'

'I'm fine,' I said, worried all over again. 'Why? Is there a reason I shouldn't be fine?' Or that I should be hiring a lawyer?

Pavlik grinned, seeming to read my mind. '*And,* I also thought I should tell you that no one genuinely suspects you of arson. It apparently just makes good convention fodder.'

'Pretty much anything does,' I said. I noticed he didn't say I wasn't suspected of murder. I decided not to bring up the subject.

Instead, I led him up the walk to the front door. 'Do you have anybody in mind for the arson?'

I thought it was unlikely that Levitt—even if he had killed LaRoche—also had burned down the coffeehouse. First of all, it was Janalee's Place. Anyone who had a personal grudge against LaRoche would have taken out a HotWired store, not Janalee's.

But second, and more importantly, LaRoche's speech apparently was what set Levitt off in the first place. Why would he commit arson *before* LaRoche had given him reason to?

Besides, burning down a building pollutes the air. It just wasn't Levitt's style. I thought he'd be more likely to introduce termites, and let nature take its course over a decade or so. But then I wouldn't have thought bean-ing LaRoche in the head was the man's style, either. Go figure.

I tuned back into what Pavlik was saying just in time to hear him say, '...some leads, but I'm letting the arson squad handle that.'

'Great,' I said as I turned the key in the door. Inside, I could hear the frantic scuffling of Frank's toenails as he dashed across the polished wood floor. I waited for the thud before I pushed the door open and peeked in.

Frank was sitting back on his haunches looking dazed. Or at least I imagined he looked dazed under all that hair.

'See?' I said, turning back to Pavlik, 'I've learned that if I wait a second or two before opening the door, I can avoid being catapulted back into the yard by the sheer force of him running into it.'

'Good thinking,' Pavlik said, following me in. He knelt down to push the hair out of Frank's eyes. 'You have trained her well,' he said to the dog. Frank tried to lick him. He missed.

'I have something I need to tell you about,' I said to Pavlik. I was holding up the covered hanger from BPG so the bottom of the dress didn't pick up dust bunnies of dog hair. 'But I really need to shower and dress first. Could you do me a huge favor and take Frank out and run him around?'

'Sure,' Pavlik said to me. To Frank, he said, 'Where's your tennis ball, go find your ball, boy, where is it where is it, huh? Huh?'

That would take care of the two of them for a good half hour.

In actuality, it took me about forty minutes to shower, dress and put on my make-up. No matter; when I looked out the window, they were still playing ball in the yard.

Time to separate man from best friend. I stepped out onto the porch.

Pavlik and Frank stopped dead.

Hey, I said to myself, I may not be a twenty-four-year-old dental floozy, but I clean up well.

That was my last lucid thought before Frank launched himself at me. Frank, in his white-and-gray fur coat, me in my black dress. This couldn't end well.

Turning, I made for the door, but Frank's big paws were already pounding up the porch steps. I felt the fetid breath of decaying beef bones and putrid pig ears hot against the back of my legs…

Then—thud, whump, WHOOSH.

I turned. Pavlik was flat on his back on the grass at the bottom of the steps, Frank on top of him, all four legs waving in the air like hairy flagpoles. I wasn't sure if the 'whoosh' had been Frank getting the wind knocked out of him or Pavlik. Neither of them looked good.

'Are you OK?' I called down, picking off a dog hair that had somehow migrated to my dress anyway.

'Mmmmph,' Pavlik said, trying to spit out a hank of Frank's fur.

I started down the steps.

'Stay!' Pavlik commanded.

I obeyed.

The sheriff had hold of Frank's collar and was trying to shimmy out from under the dog. The dog, for his part, appeared to like it.

'I think you're turning him on.'

'He's on his back, for God's sake,' Pavlik said irritably.

'You've never heard of doggy-style?'

Pavlik gave me the eye. Or he would have given me the eye, if Frank hadn't chosen just that moment to throw his head back in apparent ecstasy and pop Pavlik in the mouth.

I started forward.

'Sit.'

I sat. On the porch swing. I was hoping we were going to get to 'lay' pretty soon. I only had another fifteen minutes.

But, alas, Pavlik managed to squeeze out from under Frank. Frank rolled over and went to sleep.

'Wham, bam, thank you, Sheriff,' I contributed from my seat on the porch.

Pavlik brushed himself off. 'You *had* to wear black.'

I stood up and did a turn. 'You don't like?'

He came up the steps. 'I like very much.'

He ran his fingers over my bare shoulders. 'I only wish there was time for me to show you how much I like it.' He leaned in, his breath—smelling of neither dog bones nor pig ears—hot against my neck. 'And you.'

Sarah could wait. The banquet could wait. The whole world could wait. I pulled his lips down to mine. Pavlik's hands dropped down to encircle my waist.

'You have to go, you know,' he murmured in my hair.

'I know,' I murmured back. 'Damn, damn, damn.'

'Want a rain check?'

'Then I'll have one, and you'll have one,' I pointed out.

'God knows what could happen when two rain checks collide.'

'I think I have a pretty good idea.' I ran my index finger along his jawline to his lips. 'And if you can do that—' I nodded toward Frank, who was now snoring— 'to a sheepdog named Frank, I can't wait to see what you can do to me.'

'I'll make it worth your while, I promise,' he said, his blue eyes going dark. Dangerous man, this one.

I sighed. 'I really do have to go now, though.'

Unfortunately, he listened to me. Where are those men who drag you off to their caves, making you miss your coffee banquet, when you need them?

I stepped inside the house to get my evening bag, and then surveyed Frank. 'What am I going to do with him?'

'I'll wake him up after you're gone,' Pavlik volunteered, 'and put him in the house.'

'You are the best.' I gave him a quick kiss. 'Will you feed and water him, too? And turn on the nightlight?'

'You are high maintenance, lady. And the Tramp—' he chin-gestured to Frank— 'even more so.'

'Believe me,' I said, starting down the steps, 'I don't even begin to compare.'

I stopped when I got to the bottom. 'Oh, my God, I completely forgot.'

'What?' Pavlik seemed to be paying more attention to my retreating butt than what I was saying.

'I saw some of the video that Jerome, the college student from Brookhills Community, shot at Java Ho. He has tape of an argument between LaRoche and Levitt Fredericks after the barista competition on Friday night.'

Pavlik got out his pad and made a note. 'Great. We're starting to put a timeline together. Does the kid know about what time it is?'

'I don't know. I didn't see a time stamp or anything on the tape, but it was clearly shot as the vendors were closing down. That should help.'

Pavlik kept the notebook open. 'Just for the record, where were you Friday night?'

Something in my stomach started doing the limbo. Relax, I told it—you have an alibi. It didn't seem to care.

I cleared my throat. 'After the barista competition ended at eight, I said goodbye to everyone, including LaRoche, and went to have drinks with Kate and Jerome.'

Pavlik made a note of that. 'Until when?'

'A little after midnight.'

'Good.' Pavlik looked up and saw my face. 'Don't worry. Just routine.'

'Yeah, that's what they say in the movies, too. Just before they slap on the cuffs.'

'Actually, with the new zip-ties, it's more slipping than slapping,' he said. 'But like I said, don't worry. The medical examiner thinks LaRoche was killed between ten and midnight.'

I guess when you have 'liver temps', or whatever they used to gauge time of death, my 'Hey! He's wearing a burgundy tie!' was a little simplistic.

'Of course, that's just an estimate,' Pavlik continued. 'I'll be able to pin it down even better when I get the security tape.'

'There was a camera in the competition room?' There went all the sport in catching a killer.

'Not in the room where LaRoche was found, but I'm told there's one in the hallway leading to the side door of that room. Once the exhibit hall closed, it would be the best way in.'

'Of course, that's the door I used when...' In the nick of time, I heard a groan behind me. Frank was stirring.

'Got him.' Pavlik had jumped off the porch and had hold of Frank's collar. 'Now, what were you saying?'

'Nothing important.' I made a show of checking my watch. 'I have to run. Bye.'

As I skirted around them to the van, Pavlik dragged a recalcitrant Frank into the house.

Getting into the minivan, I sat for a moment to let my heart settle down.

How had I forgotten that I'd gone back to the competition room to check on the trophies after having drinks with Kate and Jerome?

It had to have been after midnight, because that's when the bar closed and they chased us out. I even remembered checking my watch. What time was it? Twelve fifteen? I wasn't sure.

If the time of death was between ten and twelve, though, that meant that LaRoche was already dead when

I arrived. Which also meant his body was likely under the table as I straightened the trophies and smoothed down the corner of the tablecloth.

I'd cleaned up after a murderer.

SEVENTEEN

LAROCHE'S BODY MUST have been under the table, there were no two ways about it.

It stood to reason that the table had been placed over him where he had fallen. Otherwise, there would have been blood somewhere else in the room, and I certainly hadn't seen any. There had been the spot that Sarah and I were trying to cover when we moved the table the next morning, but that definitely was not blood. It was something light in color, probably spilled during the competition.

No, I was fairly certain LaRoche was already under the table.

Then there was the other million-dollar question: why hadn't I noticed something was wrong? The murder weapon was sitting in a ring of blood. There was a body under the table, for God's sake. How could I have missed it all?

The answer was obvious. I'd had three or four glasses of wine in the bar. I was drunk. I didn't know which was scarier—that I was drunk enough not to notice a dead man, or that I had been drunk enough not to notice a dead man *and* had driven home.

It was beyond idiocy.

Ashamed of myself, I turned my attention to the road as I drove toward the convention center. Not that I could turn off the thoughts.

Had I moved the trophy that night? I didn't think so. I would have seen the blood if I had, right? Well, no—not necessarily, given everything else I'd missed. I was fairly certain, though, that 'Slut in a cup' had been right in the center of the table and I had simply left it there. That was one good thing, at least.

A sudden thought struck me. What if I *had* touched the trophy after the killer had wiped it off? Sarah's flippant suggestion that I'd grabbed it the next morning to hide the fact my prints were already on it would have seemed right on target. Would the police be able to tell when each set of prints was made? I didn't know, and I sure didn't want to ask Pavlik. Thankfully, it was a moot point now.

But speaking of Pavlik, why hadn't I just come out and told him I'd literally returned to the scene of the crime, if not *my* crime?

'Gosh, I had a party to get to' was not going to fly with the sheriff once he saw me on the security tape. Thing was, I didn't want to just blurt it out like that. I'd gotten into too much trouble in my life, saying things without thinking. So I'd thought about it—damn lot of good it did me. I still didn't know what to do.

Right now I had a banquet to manage. Focus, Maggy.

Parking in the lot outside the convention center, I slid out of the van and approached the door. The faces of the knot of smokers had changed, with the exception of one.

'It's time to go in now, Sarah,' I said gently. A woman with a black apron embroidered with the words 'Brookhills Convention Center' threw me a grateful look.

'I was just waiting for you,' Sarah protested. 'You're late.'

'I went home to change,' I said, looking her up and down. 'I see you didn't have a chance.'

If Sarah were murdered, no one would be able to determine time of death by her clothes. She wore pretty much the same thing every day. Trousers, long jacket, sensible shoes. It sounded like Katharine Hepburn, but played more like Groucho Marx.

'I accessorized.' She pointed at a pin on her lapel.

I looked closer. 'It's your Kingston Realty pin.'

'It's my dress Kingston Realty pin.' She cocked her head and took a good look at me. 'And speaking of dresses, yours is ripped.'

'It's not ripped.' I threw back my shoulders and stood tall. Mom would be so proud. 'I'm baring my shoulders.'

'Better your shoulders than those breasts of yours,' Sarah observed. 'Even with your chest thrown out like that you can't make mountains out of those molehills.'

How did she do that? How could she stand there in her everyday clothes and make me, in my slightly discounted designer dress, feel small? I could feel my chest—what there was of it—cave in and my shoulders round.

'Just kidding.' Sarah slapped me on the back. Hard. 'You look great.'

'With friends like you...' I started, but who was I kidding? Friends like her were all I had.

The banquet was to be in the Crystal Ballroom, with cocktails in the hall outside of it. The bars were scheduled to open at six thirty, which was fifteen minutes from now, but the hall was already packed.

'It looks like some people brought their own,' Sarah said, pointing at a couple in the corner with a six-pack and a pizza.

'Amazing, but not surprising.' The pepperoni and mushroom pizza looked awfully good. I couldn't remember the last time I'd eaten. 'I'm going to see if the bartenders can open early. Can you make sure everything's ready in the ballroom?'

Sarah nodded and started to walk away.

'Oh, and be sure to check the microphones,' I called after her. 'I'd hate to have LaRoche...' I stopped.

For a second there, I'd forgotten that LaRoche was dead. Now I understood why people referred to the newly dead in present tense, like they were going to walk in the door any second. While the reality might be 'dead', the brain's default position was 'alive'. Even if you didn't necessarily like the guy.

Sarah gave me a thumbs-up to show she understood and continued into the hall. I approached the nearest drink station. My bartender friend from the other night was lining up bottles of wine. One red, one white, one pink. 'Hi,' I said. 'Remember me from the other night?' And the night before that.

'You're Pinot Noir or Cab,' he said, picking up the red. 'But I'm afraid you're stuck with Merlot tonight.'

'That's fine,' I said, 'but I'm going to hold off for now. I've been put in charge of this shindig and I'd best keep a clear head.'

He nodded solemnly and set down the bottle. 'Yeah, I heard what happened. Not surprised, I have to say.'

'Really?'

'Nah.' He had started to pour a bag of ice into the cooler behind the bar and straightened up. 'Seemed like that guy always was giving someone shit.'

'Like who?' I asked curiously. 'The people who work here?'

'Pretty much everybody. Me and the other bartenders, Penny, the catering manager, the suppliers, the people trying to set up their booths. See that guy over there?'

I followed the direction he was pointing. Levitt Fredericks had just walked in the door. 'The tall guy?' I asked, just to make sure.

'Yeah, I thought he was going to kill him the other day.'

'That Levitt was going to kill him?' I tried to keep my voice down, but I was excited. It was a relief to know I was on the right track.

But the bartender—his name tag said George— looked confused. 'I thought his name was "LayRochay". French or something.'

Something. 'No, I meant Levitt Fredericks,' I clarified. 'He's the tall gray-haired man you just pointed at.'

George wiped at the bar. 'I have to take your word for it that's his name. But it was the other guy, the guy that was killed, who was threatening the old guy.'

Wait a second. Marvin LaRoche was angry at Levitt Fredericks? That didn't track. 'Did you hear what they were arguing about?'

'Just this LayRochay guy telling your friend to "stay away from her".' George shrugged. 'Listen, it's six thirty. I gotta open up here.'

So much for opening the bars early. My new friends, the two gray-haired women, were at the front of the line and looking daggers at me.

I thanked the bartender and started to walk away. Then I thought of something. Actually, two somethings. 'Do you remember what night that was?'

'Not night,' he said, making a scotch and water. 'It was late afternoon on Thursday. I remember because we were setting up the bars before that big opening reception of yours.'

'Afternoon,' I said. 'You're sure.'

'Absolutemently.' He started work on the second drink, a screwdriver.

I began to walk away again. Thursday afternoon— that was before LaRoche's speech. Why were they arguing then? Did LaRoche attack EarthBean's mission during that speech in retaliation for something else? Something that had started far earlier?

I turned back. 'One last thing. Did you hear a name? The name of the woman they were talking about?'

George paused, the old ladies' change in hand. I thought one of them—I was starting to think of them as The Pigeon Sisters—was going to leap over the bar to get it.

'The old guy said…' George closed his eyes to recall the exact words. 'He…said, "I can't, I need her."'

'And the other guy, the dead guy said, "Well, she sure as hell doesn't need you."' George was acting it out now, doing the voices. Even the Pigeons were transfixed.

'And then the old guy says something like, "I'll die without her."'

This was way more than I expected. I should talk to bartenders more often. '"Her" who?' I demanded.

George's hand was placed dramatically over his heart and he closed his eyes. 'He didn't say, but then the dead guy says, "Then die."'

There was a hush, and George opened one eye.

'The name,' I begged. 'Did he say a name?'

'Yup.' George handed a Pigeon Sister her change. She looked loath to leave at this point. 'I remember it because it's my mother's name.'

It's always their mother's name. 'And your mother's name is?'

George popped the top off a Miller Lite for the next customer and handed it to him over the heads of the still-transfixed Pigeons.

'Amy,' he said, taking the bills from the beer drinker. 'My mother's name is Amy.'

I PICKED MY WAY through the crowd toward the Crystal Ballroom. The doors would be shut until we let people in at seven thirty and I could really use some time to think.

Amy and Levitt?

Levitt had about a foot in height and thirty years in age over Amy. Not that either of those things could stop true love. Or lust.

But still...THUD. I'd just collided head-on with Antonio. He was looking very handsome in a dark gray suit, and under any other circumstances, I would have taken some time to enjoy it.

'I am very sorry, Maggy. Pardon me,' Antonio said, a twinkle in his dark eyes. 'I was not looking where I am going.'

'I'm afraid it was my fault, Antonio, but thank you.'

He smiled down at me. 'I understand that you have taken over the management of Java Ho. That is very kind of you.'

'I did it to help Janalee,' I said honestly.

'She will need her friends now,' he said. 'Her husband was a powerful businessman. But he was still a man. And we men have many weaknesses.'

I wasn't sure what he was getting at, but something he said switched on a lightbulb. LaRoche being human, that was it.

'I saw you talking to him that night after the barista competition,' I said. 'I thought he might be crying.'

Antonio cocked his head. 'I would be surprised at that.'

I waited a moment for him to add something. Anything. He didn't, so I moved on to *other* men's weaknesses. 'So Antonio, have you heard anything about a relationship between Amy and Levitt Fredericks?'

A hesitation, then: 'A gentlemen never tells,' he said gently, but firmly.

And Antonio was a gentleman, so much so that gossiping with him was nigh impossible. Not to mention, downright humiliating. I could feel myself color up with embarrassment at having asked the question.

'A casual friendship, a great love.' Antonio shrugged expressively. 'Who are we on the outside to know?'

'Well, OK, then,' I said, clearing my throat uncomfortably. 'I have to check the ballroom now. You have a good time.'

And with that, I slipped through the doors.

OUT OF THE FRYING PAN and into the fire. Sarah's fire.

'Good news,' she yelled across the tables when she saw me. 'You don't have to worry about the microphone.'

'Great,' I said, surveying the room set-up. Luckily, not all of the Java Ho attendees sprang for the banquet. There should be sixty rounds of eight, totaling 480 seats. I counted one row and then multiplied. Yup, all there—first obstacle hurdled.

A woman was going from table to table affixing a yellow sticker under one chair at each table. The lucky winner would get to take home the centerpiece, which was a fancy basket filled with five separate one-pound bags of coffee beans from various roasters. The roasters donated the beans as a way of showing off their coffees to the coffeehouse owners. If the owners were anything like me, though, the last thing they wanted to see by now was another pound of coffee.

Each table was covered in white linen like the trophy table had been. I wondered how much they spent on bleach in this place. The sticker-lady straightened up when she saw me. 'Excuse me. Are you Maggy Thorsen?'

I stuck out my hand. 'Yes, and I bet you're Penny.' The woman had copper-colored hair, so it was a safe guess. What wasn't so obvious was whether the hair color or the name had come first.

'I'm so sorry,' Penny said, holding my hand between both of hers.

'Thank you,' I said. 'LaRoche's death was a shock to all of us.'

Sarah had come up to us. 'She's not talking about the murder.'

Uh-oh. I looked around. A thousand things could go wrong with a banquet. The tables and chairs were obviously there, and the waitresses were setting out the salads. That left the main course, or...

'The sound system.' I turned to Sarah. 'I thought you said I didn't have to worry about the microphones.'

'You don't,' she said. 'There aren't any.'

'There aren't any?' I repeated, looking at Penny. The hair color must be natural, because her face pretty much matched it now.

'That's not exactly true,' she said. 'We do have microphones.'

'Just nothing to plug them into,' Sarah contributed.

'No, no, that's really not true either,' Penny said, bobbing her head from side to side. 'The problem is that anything spoken into the microphone here is broadcast throughout the entire building, for some reason.'

The entire building was not my problem. 'I think we can live with that,' I said pleasantly. 'Then people in the bathroom won't have to miss any of the speeches.' You can run, but you can't hide.

'Well, see—' Penny tugged at her nose— 'Java Ho isn't the only function in the building.'

'But it's the *biggest* function, right?' Years of doing corporate events meant I wasn't averse to pulling rank.

'But it's a wedding.' Penny looked like she was going to cry. 'They're just the nicest young couple.'

Yeah, well nineteen and a half years of marriage would cure that, take it from me. 'So what can we do to fix this?' I asked in the spirit of cooperation.

Penny shot me a grateful look. 'We have a portable sound system we can bring in.'

'Is it powerful enough for this room?' We were talking about a pretty big space with high ceilings.

'It has two huge speakers. We can position one on each side of the stage. Our engineer is bringing them up now.'

'Good,' I said, looking at the lectern centered on the stage. 'Will the system tie into the microphone on the lectern?'

'I believe so,' Penny said, 'but here's our engineer now. He can tell you for sure.'

The engineer, a man of about forty-five with salt-and-pepper hair, left the flatbed truck he'd just rolled in and came over to us.

'Mike,' Penny said, 'this is Maggy Thorsen. She was asking if the sound system will use the lectern microphone.'

'It will,' he said.

Out of nowhere, Sarah jumped in. 'My only concern is that if you turn your head while you're speaking, the fixed directional mic doesn't pick you up.'

I turned to look at her in amazement. The speech-maker finally surfaces. *And* apparently Sarah had found someone who spoke her own language. It didn't hurt that he was good-looking and wasn't wearing a wedding ring.

'You're right,' Mike agreed with a smile. 'Lavalieres would be better, because they pin on your lapel.'

He nodded at Sarah, who actually had a lapel. I looked down at my dress. A pin-on microphone would absolutely ruin my outfit. Not to mention that a Lavaliere—like the one I'd had on for the aborted finals of the barista competition—has that pesky wire snaked through under your clothes to connect to the pack on your belt.

You guessed it: no belt.

And no one was going to be snaking *any*thing up under my dress unless it was Pavlik.

Happily, I didn't plan on doing much talking anyway.

'The problem with the Lavs,' Mike was saying to Sarah, who looked fascinated, 'is they're not compatible with the portable sound system we have to use. I assume you're one of the speakers?'

Sarah nodded; if it weren't Sarah, I would have said she did so demurely.

The engineer moved over to her. 'The speeches are at what time?'

'The sooner the better,' I said, and they both looked at me like I'd crashed a private party. 'Probably eight fifteen, eight thirty,' I added lamely.

Mike looked back at Sarah. 'Tell you what I can do for you. After I set this up, I'll hook you up with the Lav.'

'We have another speaker, too,' I interjected, waving my hand like I was asking permission to speak. 'Levitt Fredericks.'

Mike turned and Sarah mouthed, 'Butt out' to me, behind his back.

'No,' I said.

Mike looked confused. 'No?'

'I meant no one else, just Sarah and Levitt.'

'Then I can wire up both of them. The Lavs won't work with the portable system, but if I get whatever is crossed uncrossed before your speeches, you'll be all set to go.'

He looked at Sarah. 'I'll just give you the high sign.'

'I'd like that,' Sarah said.

That was it. I was going to puke. 'He wasn't talking about *that* high sign,' I told Sarah. 'And Mike, thank you for whatever you can do.'

Penny, seeing we were in handsome hands, had gone back to her stickers. 'It's seven twenty-five,' I called to her. 'Will we be ready to open the doors in five minutes?'

She straightened up. 'We're ready if you're ready.'

I was ready, all right. Ready to get this over with. But like I said, be careful what you wish for.

EIGHTEEN

THE FIRST SHOCK of the evening was that Janalee was there.

The second shock was that Davy wasn't.

When I saw Janalee, I flagged her down and asked her to sit with us at the head table.

'You belong here,' I pointed out when she hesitated. 'You would have sat here before. You should sit here now.'

'I wouldn't be too sure,' she said, with a little smile. 'Marvin said if I brought Davy, I was going to be relegated to a table at the back of the room.'

'Is that why you didn't bring the baby?' I asked. 'Because Marvin asked you not to, before he died?' I thought that was sweet on Janalee's part, and understandable on LaRoche's. Babies don't belong at banquets. They should be home having fun like the rest of us want to be.

'Truthfully?' Janalee said the word like it was a real question, not just a segue or a figure of speech.

I nodded.

She leaned in. 'I had every intention of bringing Davy just to irritate Marvin.' She gave a little giggle and then quickly covered her mouth, looking around to see if anyone had heard. 'It was my way of keeping him in line,' she added in a whisper.

I liked that. And I liked Janalee—even if she did seem a little tipsy tonight. God knows I'd be drinking if I were in her place. 'So why didn't you bring Davy, then?'

'It was a silly little game I played,' she said with a little sigh. 'It just didn't seem so important anymore.'

Geez. I didn't even like LaRoche and this was getting me choked up. Any minute now I'd be referring to him as Marvin.

Nah.

'There's Amy,' Janalee said, pointing. 'Do you think we have room for her at the table?'

I did a quick calculation. Janalee, Levitt, Sarah, me. We still had half a table to fill. 'Of course.' I waved at Amy, who had stopped to talk to Antonio, and signaled that they both should join us.

As they approached, I scanned the room for other people to invite to the table. Jerome was at the far end of the hall taping. Kate still seemed to be overseeing him, which made me a little nervous. Without a barista competition, I imagined she was there as a reporter. And like I said, that made me nervous.

'Great dress, Maggy,' Amy said, as she and Antonio came up to us. 'Very chic.'

'Thank you,' I said, 'but I think you have me beat.'

Amy did a little pirouette. She was wearing a short green satin dress and looked spectacular.

'Thanks. We're all wearing green as a show of solidarity.' She pointed over to Levitt, who was wearing a black suit with a forest-green shirt-and-tie combination.

I assumed 'we' was EarthBean, and the 'show of solidarity' was in response to LaRoche's speech. But with LaRoche dead, wasn't the show of solidarity a little insensitive?

I glanced over to Janalee to see if she was feeling uncomfortable, but she seemed just fine. In fact, now that I looked, I saw that she was wearing green, too—an emerald brooch that lent the only hint of color to her black dress. She might be in mourning, but she was also in support of EarthBean, or so it appeared.

'Where's Davy?' Amy asked, glancing around like she expected to see him crawling amongst the tables. Given her considerable experience with Janalee's parenting, that was understandable.

Janalee laughed. 'Amy knows that she's the only person in town I'll leave Davy with.'

'Janalee doesn't trust anyone else with him,' Amy said with a little smile.

'I can't imagine anyone better,' Antonio said charmingly, looking appreciatively at Amy's legs.

You know, much as I was partial to Pavlik's blue-to-gray eyes, Antonio's dark ones boring into you were enough to make a woman want to pull off her clothes and...

'My mother came this afternoon to stay with us for a while, and she's watching Davy,' Janalee told Amy.

'*Who's* watching Davy?' a voice behind me said. When I turned, I saw Kate with her notepad out, and Jerome at her right elbow.

'On duty, Kate?' I asked, not bothering to answer her question.

'I'm a reporter, Maggy,' she said coolly. 'I'm always on duty.'

Oh, pleeeze. I saw Penny hovering and took the opportunity to get away from Kate.

'I don't mean to interrupt,' Penny said when I joined her, 'but could you get everyone to sit down and start on their salads?'

'Of course,' I said, looking around for Sarah. I had intended to make her do all the announcements, but she was probably in the electrical closet with the engineer. 'Is the sound system all set?' I asked Penny.

'Yes, and Mike is getting Ms Kingston wired.'

'I wouldn't be at all surprised,' I said, and walked up to the lectern. I came this close to saying, 'Is this on?' but satisfied myself with a simple: 'Would everyone please take their seats?'

By the time I got back to the table, Kate and Jerome were gone and my group was obediently seated. Three chairs stood empty. Two to the right of Sarah and one to her left, between her and Antonio.

Despite the fact that apparently no one wanted to sit next to her, Sarah was looking pretty pleased with herself.

'All "Miked" up?' I asked, taking the seat to her immediate right.

'That's beneath you, Maggy,' she said, but she couldn't quite keep the grin off her face.

A waiter came over to the table with two bottles of wine—one red and one white. It wasn't a bad idea, but I didn't think we'd ordered it and told him so.

'Compliments of the management,' he said. 'In apology for the—' he consulted a note— 'little engineering glitch.'

Sarah giggled, a sound not often heard in nature. I followed her gaze and saw Mike across the room. Ahh, the engineer wants her liquored up. Who was I to stand in the way of true love?

'I'll take the red,' I said. One glass and no more, I promised myself. I had to drive home, after all.

Amy declined, as did Levitt next to her. I wondered if there was such a thing as organic wine. Antonio had a glass of the Merlot, while Sarah asked for the white. I figured it was because it looked more like vodka than the red.

'You don't drink wine,' I said to her.

'You don't know *every*thing about me.' She took a sip of the wine and involuntarily grimaced before plastering a smile on her face. The smile had to be for the engineer. She sure didn't care what the rest of us thought.

'I'm breastfeeding,' Janalee was volunteering to the waiter, putting her hand over her glass to prevent him from pouring.

'Still?' Sarah said, neatly diverting the subject from herself. 'Doesn't that kid have teeth?'

If Sarah's choppers ran in the family, I could understand her horror. Still, I'd breastfed Eric for a while and started to come to Janalee's defense. Then I thought better of it. There was something about having a smoky Italian at the table that made one not want to talk about breastfeeding. Or hot flashes. Period.

Antonio didn't seem to mind, though. 'I think it's charming that women breastfeed. Very nurturing,' he was saying.

I wasn't paying much attention, though, because I had just seen a familiar face enter the room.

'Pavlik?' I said, under my breath.

'What about Pavlik?' Sarah asked, gingerly taking another sip of wine. 'And when are you going to call the guy by his first name?' She hesitated. 'What is it again?'

'It's Jake,' I hissed, 'and he's here.'

'Here?' Sarah looked around. 'So he is. Think he's going to arrest someone?'

'Hope so,' I said, trying to feign unconcern. 'Then we can cancel this damn banquet.' I took a healthy gulp of wine as I watched Pavlik thread his way through the tables.

Sarah pulled out her puffer and took a hit. 'Especially awkward if it's you,' she said.

Which was exactly what I was thinking, of course. Pavlik had seen the tape from the hall outside the competition room. And he had seen me on that tape. He was coming to get me.

I stood up and started toward him, figuring I'd save myself the humiliation of being handcuffed at the head table. The sheriff just waved me back and kept coming. He was wearing a dark suit. Not his usual arresting attire.

'Sorry to be late,' he said, giving me a kiss on the cheek.

'Maggy,' Sarah said archly from beside me. 'Where are your manners? Introduce Sheriff Pavlik to everyone.'

'I think the sheriff knows everyone,' I said. 'You know, from the, um…'

'Not everyone,' Pavlik said. He stuck out his hand to Antonio. 'I'm Jake Pavlik.'

Antonio stood up. 'A pleasure, Sheriff. I am Antonio Silva.'

'You're The Milkman,' Pavlik said pleasantly. 'Maggy has mentioned you.'

In fact, I hadn't. Ever. I prefer to keep my fantasy lovers compartmentalized. Pavlik in the 'a real possibility' box, Antonio in the 'fun to think about' box.

So what was Pavlik up to?

He was smiling at Janalee. 'Good to see you out, Mrs LaRoche.'

Had to hand it to him. Pavlik's statement didn't have a whiff of 'Why are you partying the night after your husband was killed, you unfeeling bitch?'

Still it won him an explanation.

'I told her she needed to be with her friends,' Amy piped up.

Janalee smiled. 'And you were right, Amy.' She turned to Pavlik. 'The coffee community is a very small one, and we depend on each other to a much bigger degree than even we realize.'

'Really?' By now Pavlik was seated on my right, next to Levitt. He waved over the guy with the wine.

'It's true,' Levitt said, nodding. The wine guy, thinking he was nodding to him, filled his glass. 'Oh, no, I meant…'

He picked up the filled glass, trying to get the man's attention. Failing in that, he set it back on the table and pushed it away from him before he continued.

'What I meant was that Janalee is right. Store owners—' he nodded at Janalee and me— 'and suppliers like Antonio do well when specialty coffee does well.'

Pavlik glanced over at me. His eyes were dark, nearly black, with the look he gets when he's extremely focused. At first I thought it was directed toward me, then he turned to Levitt.

'Surely, that can't be true of you,' he said. 'EarthBean is a watchdog group. Though I suppose a case could be made that you wouldn't have a job without people like LaRoche.'

'My job, quite honestly, would be much easier without people like…' He broke off and raised his hand apologetically to Janalee.

Janalee shook her head. 'It's all right, Levitt. I know that Marvin double-crossed you.'

She turned to Pavlik. 'You see, Marvin had promised his support toward a program providing a living wage to coffee-growers in Central America.'

'What happened?' Pavlik asked.

'He withdrew his support.' Levitt was running his thumb and forefinger up and down the stem of the wineglass. Amy, apparently fearing he was going to spill it, made a stab at moving it away from the edge, but Levitt ignored her. 'It was bad enough that LaRoche didn't come through, himself, but he also incited other people to do the same.'

'In his opening speech?' Pavlik asked.

Levitt took a swig of his wine. 'That's correct.'

'So was that what you were arguing with him about on Friday night?'

Levitt looked up sharply. 'Where did you hear that?'

I'd been so busy worrying about the camera I was afraid I'd been caught on, that I'd forgotten about the one that Levitt certainly was on. Jerome's.

'Oh, look,' I said brightly, 'they're bringing dinner!'

'Chicken,' Sarah murmured in my ear. I didn't think she was talking about the entrée.

'I didn't just hear it,' Pavlik was telling Levitt, 'I saw it. On tape.'

Since I'd left him at my house, Pavlik couldn't have tracked Jerome down for the tape, watched it, and still had time to change clothes and get here to crash the party. The sheriff was on a fishing expedition. And I had provided the bait.

Under Pavlik's scrutiny, Levitt was getting serious about his wine. 'I told him that people were starving. That they were living in poverty.'

'What did he say?' Pavlik asked.

'He said, "If everyone took care of their own, we wouldn't need groups like EarthBean to hand out charity."'

'Didn't Ebenezer Scrooge say something like that?' Sarah said in my ear.

I rubbed at the ear. 'Eat your chicken,' I whispered back, as my keynote speaker downed the rest of his wine and signaled the waiter for another.

Amy jumped in. 'That's ridiculous. EarthBean doesn't hand out charity, we—'

Levitt waved her down. 'It makes no matter what the truth is, Amy. If the perception of the industry—'

'And LaRoche speaks for the industry?' Pavlik asked.

'No. LaRoche spoke for LaRoche.' Levitt was getting loud and no longer sounding much like a southern gentleman. Or a gentleman of any kind. 'The bastard had a big mouth, and he was goddamn power hungry. People like that make themselves heard. They lead the people who are too weak or too stupid to find the way themselves.'

Levitt had said the last bit seemingly at the top of his lungs and the people at the tables surrounding us were turning. I glanced around for Kate. She and Jerome were just three tables away and she was whispering in his ear and pointing. Probably instructing him to go paparazzi on us. When Kate saw me looking, she gave a little wave and a smile.

Meanwhile, Levitt had drained his second glass and was working on Pavlik's wine. I couldn't put this guy on the podium.

I turned to Sarah beseechingly. She nodded and stood up. 'I'll take care of this.'

Sarah stepped to the lectern. Hesitating for a second, she glanced off into the far corner of the room and nodded. Mike the engineer must have been letting her know the Lavaliere microphones were working.

'Excuse me,' she said, not bothering with the fixed mic on the lectern. 'I know we're all anxious to get on with the evening, so I thought we'd start as you finish eating.'

Jerome had hustled up to the front of the room and fixed his camera on her.

SANDRA BALZO
185

Sarah smiled into it. 'I'm Sarah Kingston, and I've been asked to say a few words about the chairman of this year's Java Ho: Marvin LaRoche.'

She cleared her throat and waited for the little buzz that had started at the mention of LaRoche's name to settle down. 'Some people loved Marvin LaRoche—' she nodded to Janalee— 'and some people hated him.' The buzz grew.

Sarah waved it down. 'But the fact is, people, he's dead. Get over it.'

Aww geez, could this get any worse?

'And now, here's our keynote speaker, Levitt Fredericks.'

What was Sarah doing? She was supposed to be getting me out of this fix. If Levitt got to the lectern in his condition, it would be a nightmare. A really long, rambling nightmare.

I tried to lean across Pavlik to tell Levitt to stay where he was, but the gray-haired man was already getting up.

Then a higher power—in this case, duct tape—intervened. As Levitt scooted his chair back, the legs caught on the duct tape that pieced the carpet together. The chair toppled backwards, Levitt in it.

'Oh, thank God,' I said, before I could stop myself. Even Sarah looked shocked. I was going to hell.

Or maybe we were already in hell, because right then Levitt—his Lavaliere mic now live—let loose with a string of curse words, the likes of which I'd never heard. And I had a teenage son.

On the bright side, under the overturned chair was a yellow sticker. Guess who was taking home the centerpiece.

NINETEEN

'WHAT IN THE WORLD were you two thinking?' I said, setting down my glass of wine.

'Who two?' Pavlik asked.

We were in my living room on the couch. It wasn't nearly as cozy as it sounds.

'You and Sarah,' I said. 'You questioning Levitt in a public place, surrounded by the people involved—including the victim's wife, for God's sake. Isn't that against the rules or something?'

'What rules?' Pavlik asked mildly.

'I don't know what rules,' I said, tucking my feet up under me. 'Interrogation Techniques 101?'

'I thought it was pretty effective.'

I punched him. 'And who invited you anyway? Walking in there, acting like you were my date,' I muttered.

'I wouldn't have had to act if you'd invited me.' His eyes were bright blue and dancing. I would have taken advantage of those eyes under any other circumstances. Not to mention the curly black hair and the pecs under the dress shirt.

'You used me.'

'You're pouting,' he said, touching my bottom lip. 'You could hang a bucket on that lip.'

I shoved his hand away. 'And then Sarah betrays me. I thought she was going to bail me out and, instead, after *you* get Levitt drunk and belligerent, Sarah calls him up to the stage.'

'He was your keynote speaker after all.'

'You know what I don't understand?' I continued. 'I don't understand how he got drunk so fast. First he's not drinking, then he downs three glasses of wine in five minutes flat.

'I'll tell you one thing,' I said, now on a roll. 'George was dead-on right about something going on between Amy and Levitt. Did you see how she was fussing over him? I think she took him home.'

'Well, he certainly was in no condition to drive,' Pavlik said soberly. 'Who's George?'

'The bartender. He told me he heard Levitt and La-Roche arguing on Thursday afternoon.'

'Thursday afternoon?' As if by magic, Pavlik had a notepad out.

Remind me not to say something probative during sex—if we ever get around to having it. I'd end up with paper cuts.

'And they were arguing about Amy?' Pavlik asked.

'George said it sounded like LaRoche was warning Levitt to stay away from Amy. Levitt, in turn, was saying he couldn't live without her.'

Pavlik paused in his writing. 'Pretty theatrical stuff. You sure George the bartender didn't make it up?'

'I don't think so,' I said, picking up my wineglass and swishing it. 'He was making a screwdriver when he said it.'

Pavlik tipped his head down to look at me and a lock of hair fell down over his forehead. 'And the screwdriver means what?'

'That he was working and distracted,' I said. 'He wasn't sitting around making up stories, he was just telling me what he remembered.'

'Right. One doesn't mess with orange juice and vodka.' Pavlik made another note. 'So why would La-Roche care if anything was going on between Levitt and Amy?'

'Well, Amy's quite a bit younger than either Levitt or LaRoche,' I said. 'Maybe her boss was simply being protective.'

Pavlik and I looked at each other.

'Nah,' we said simultaneously. Caron had heard there was 'friction' between LaRoche and Amy. Little did she know how right she might be.

'Wonder if his wife knew,' Pavlik followed up.

'And decided to kill him?' I shook my head. 'I don't know. After talking to Janalee tonight, I don't think she cared passionately enough about LaRoche to kill him, even if she did find out he was fooling around.

'Torture him a little,' I added, almost to myself. 'But not kill him.'

'Personal experience?' Pavlik probed lightly.

'Mine?' I asked, startled.

'Yes.' Pavlik moved a little closer. 'You've never told me much about your divorce.'

The last thing I wanted to do was go on a side-excursion through Ted-Ville, the part of my brain where I'd stuffed my ex. Five or six brain cells were all I was willing to spend on him at this point and—to my surprise—it was getting fewer every day.

'The divorce was very amicable,' I said, drawing myself up taller. 'And yours?' What's sauce for the goose, and all that rot.

'Completely amicable,' Pavlik said with a grin.

'I'm glad.' I was lying through my teeth and hoping he was doing likewise.

'OK, I'll add possible love triangle to the list,' Pavlik said, snapping his notebook shut. 'God knows there seem to be enough people who wanted to kill LaRoche.'

'Yet he seemed oblivious to it,' I mused. 'I don't think he had any idea people didn't like him.'

'Might have made him an easy target, then. He probably never suspected anyone would want to harm him.'

I thought of LaRoche, his ego and his idol, Sun Tzu. 'Or dare to. And even if he did, I think he would assume he would prevail because he was smarter, braver and tougher than everyone else.'

'Except one cheap trophy.'

I ignored the insult to 'Slut in a cup'. He was right, in more ways than one.

Pavlik stood up. 'By the way,' he said, tucking his pen away, 'I got a look at that tape from the back hallway.'

A chill went up my back. I was familiar enough with Pavlik to know this wasn't an afterthought.

'Is this our Columbo moment?' I asked.

'Please?'

'You know, where the deceptively bumbling detective stops at the door and asks the "oh, by the way" question, thereby cutting, laser-like, to the heart of the matter?'

But Pavlik hadn't gotten past the first part of my compound question. 'Bumbling?' He leaned down to kiss me. It was a very thorough kiss.

'I said, "deceptively bumbling",' I murmured after he'd finished.

'So why didn't you tell me?' he asked, getting serious. His eyes were dark again and he was towering over me, since I was still sitting on the couch. Quintessential Pavlik. I needed to regain equal footing. Retake the hill. Level the playing field. Whatever.

I patted the couch next to me and he sat back down. Victory.

'I didn't volunteer the information at first,' I told him, 'because I honestly had forgotten.'

'You forgot that you visited the scene of the crime right around the time it was committed?' He sounded skeptical and who could blame him?

'I'd had drinks with Kate and Jerome, the camera operator,' I said lamely.

'I'd say you had one drink too many,' Pavlik observed.

'You're right,' I said, getting hot. And not in the good way. 'But I just stopped in the competition room on my way out to check the trophies.'

'What time was that?'

'Just after midnight. The smaller trophies were on the table, bunched in the center around the…'

'Murder weapon,' Pavlik supplied.

'Yeah, that.'

'Was the table where you found it the next morning? Or don't you remember?'

I ignored the jibe. 'Yes, but one corner of the tablecloth was up. I smoothed it down.'

Pavlik frowned. 'That was careless.'

'I didn't mean to destroy evidence,' I said, nervously picking up my wineglass and setting it back down again.

'No.' Pavlik had the ubiquitous notebook out again. 'It was careless of the murderer to leave the corner up.'

'That's true,' I said, grateful for the reprieve. 'The killer had to move the table to cover the body. That's why the trophies were in the middle. So they wouldn't fall off the table when he moved it.' I looked at Pavlik. 'So why would he go to all that trouble and leave without making sure the cloth was down?'

'Maybe he—or she—didn't leave.'

I put my hand to my mouth as I realized what he was driving at. 'The killer was still there when I walked in?'

'Don't know.' Pavlik shrugged. 'Would you have noticed if he was?'

I gave him a dirty look. 'Nice. But I like to think I would have felt some sort of…presence.'

'That's only in the movies,' Pavlik said, standing up and tucking the notebook away for what I hoped was the last time. 'In real life, we're too busy with our own thoughts to pay much attention to other people, much less "presences". The competition room is big and there are bleachers and dividers in it. The killer could have been hiding anywhere.'

It was true that I'd been so preoccupied with Kate's accusation about the fire at Janalee's Place, that there could have been a Tyrannosaurus rex in the room and I wouldn't have noticed. I hadn't noticed a body, for God's sake. A body that must have been just inches from my feet.

I shivered. 'It had just happened. If I interrupted the murderer, then it had just happened. That's why.' I was talking to myself.

'Why what?'

Astonished at my own stupidity, I looked up at him. 'Why I didn't smell anything. No bowel or bladder smell, nothing.'

'Hmm.' Pavlik was probably remembering another body I'd stumbled across, where just the opposite was true. But that's another story.

'On the other hand,' I continued, 'I did notice something this morning. I just figured Davy had another stinky diaper from all the nuts and berries, or whatever Janalee feeds him.'

'Maybe—' Pavlik started to say, but I interrupted.

'*Maybe* he wasn't dead at all,' I finished for him. I stood up and looked Pavlik in the eye. 'Maybe LaRoche was still alive under that table.'

The sheriff shook his head. 'Don't beat yourself up about that, at least. His skull was crushed in. If he was alive, it wasn't for long.'

'If only I had looked under that table when I fixed the tablecloth,' I said, rubbing my own forehead. 'It would have been a natural thing to do.'

Pavlik took me by the shoulders. 'And then maybe it would have been natural for the assailant to kill you, too.'

There was that.

'I get it.' I said. 'OK.'

Pavlik let go and started putting on his jacket.

I trailed him to the door. 'So when you saw me on that tape, did you seriously think I had murdered LaRoche?' It seemed an important question to ask of someone you want a relationship with.

'Tape?' Pavlik said absently as he opened the door.

'The tape from the camera outside the competition room,' I said.

'Don't be silly.' He kissed me hard on the lips. 'Why would there be a camera in that hallway and nowhere else in the convention center?' He winked at me and was gone.

Pavlik had reeled me in, just like he had Levitt Fredericks. And I hadn't even put up much of a fight.

Maybe there were worse things than never having sex.

With the sheriff in the house, the thought of someone lurking behind the bleachers in the competition room last night was manageable.

Frank's presence didn't inspire quite that much confidence.

'You would protect me, wouldn't you, boy?' I asked, picking up what was left of my wine and slipping down onto the floor next to him.

Frank, sprawled out in front of the cold fireplace, raised his head, presumably to look at me. The look said 'I'm here for you' and 'I can't see a damn thing' all rolled into one.

I sighed and flipped over on my back, head resting on Frank's furry shoulder. The night was chilly damp and I thought about tossing a log on the fireplace. Finding a match to light the paper wrapper of my fake log seemed like too much work, though. 'Go fetch a match, Frank.'

He didn't answer.

'Lazy,' I chastised him. I thought about getting another glass of wine, but it would require opening a new bottle. 'Don't suppose you have a corkscrew under there, do you, boy?' I asked, moving aside some fur.

I got a snore in response.

Eric should have gotten a St Bernard.

I was feeling a little batty with equal parts of wine, fear and regret. The thought that LaRoche was dying under the table while I was playing with the trophies was horrifying. Equally so was that the killer—likely someone I knew—could have been there watching me. Might still be watching me.

After all, how would he know if I'd seen anything that could incriminate him? And what would he do if he thought I had? I gave a shiver and Frank groaned.

Focus on what you know, Maggy, I told myself. Not on what you're afraid someone else might know.

So what did I know?

I knew that LaRoche had been killed with a trophy, in the competition room by...Colonel Mustard.

I giggled.

No, seriously. The facts.

Presumably, LaRoche had been attacked just before I arrived just after midnight. So why was he there that late? In fact, why was he there at all?

'I'm the one who should have been there, if anybody,' I said out loud. 'I was in charge of the competition.'

Frank didn't respond, but a shiver ran down my spine.
'No, really,' I said, sitting up and giving Frank a little
shake. 'Maybe I was the one who was supposed to be
killed?'

Frank lifted his head. He looked cynical.

'True,' I said, settling back down against him. 'No
one would expect me to return to the hall in the middle
of the night.' Certainly no one who knew me, at least.

That still didn't explain why LaRoche was there.

To meet someone? Maybe Amy? I thought about the
possibility. Ever since my husband Ted had drilled his
dental hygienist, I was usually the first one to suspect
hanky-panky. But even if something were going on between LaRoche and Amy, why would they meet in the
convention center? Amy wasn't married. They could
have gone to her place.

So what other business could LaRoche have had in
the competition room? What was there, after all, except
for the stage and bleachers and the competitors' supplies
and equipment?

That stopped me. LaRoche was wildly competitive,
fancying himself a strategist à la Sun Tzu. And, as Levitt
had said, the HotWired owner believed in taking care
of his own. In the context of the battle for best barista,
'his own' were Janalee and Amy.

Had LaRoche been in the hall trying to sabotage the
other competitors?

If so, how would he have done it? The three sets
of equipment had to be shared by the competitors. He
would have no way of knowing which of the three set-
ups Amy and Janalee would be assigned. Heck, I hadn't
even decided that.

So maybe the supplies?

Each competitor had a cart for their equipment, china and non-perishables and refrigerator space for dairy products and the like. LaRoche wouldn't know whose was whose there, either. I had a good idea, but I'd been much more intimately involved in the competition than LaRoche.

'And what was he going to do anyway?' I asked Frank. 'Curdle their milk?'

Frank didn't bother to answer.

He was right. The idea was a non-starter.

So, maybe LaRoche was lured to the competition room by someone. Someone who thought killing the guy with his own convention's trophy was not only appropriate, but symbolic.

Someone like Levitt Fredericks.

There was certainly no love lost between Levitt and LaRoche. Levitt had made that pretty clear before he passed out at dinner. And a lovers' triangle between Levitt, LaRoche and Amy added a whole new wrinkle.

So, Levitt had lured LaRoche there to kill him.

Or LaRoche had lured Levitt there, and Levitt had killed him in self-defense.

'That would be my choice,' I said out loud. 'If that was how it played out, maybe everybody can still live happily ever after.' Except for LaRoche, of course.

Frank gave a little whimper, then a bark, a low growl and another whimper. His legs bicycled.

'Puppy dreams, huh?' I gave him a little rub behind the ears. 'Must be nice to dream about running through fields and chasing rabbits.'

Lately my dreams had been more of the 'being chased by giant-breasted baristas' variety. That and the 'drowning in a sea of debt' dream. But then who doesn't have that one?

'Sleep, I fear, won't come easily tonight,' I told Frank, patting what felt like his head. With a sigh, I got up, checked my cellphone for messages, and slipped a movie in the DVD player.

IN MY DREAM, I'm in Uncommon Grounds. There's a 'Barista Wanted' sign in the window and a customer sitting at the counter, sipping coffee. I'm on the other side of the counter, wiping it down with a rag.

Neither one of us seems to notice the body on the floor. It's Marvin LaRoche, eyes fixed and staring at a mobile—the kind that hangs over a baby's crib—on the ceiling above. Suspended from the center of the mobile is a miniature 'Slut in a cup', surrounded by five runner-up trophies.

The chimes on the door jangle, and a woman comes in. I look up. The woman has rainbow-colored hair. Amy.

'I see you want a man,' she says.

I shake my head 'no' and start to point to the 'Barista Wanted' sign in the window.

Except now it says 'Man Wanted'.

The chimes again, and in comes Janalee. She's wearing a black suit. In mourning. She has baby spit on one shoulder and is carrying Davy. In Davy's mouth is a pacifier. It's in the shape of a toy soldier.

'Looking for a job?' I ask Amy, as I toss Janalee the rag to wipe the spit off her shoulder.

'No, a man.' She shrugs. 'I never like any I've ever had. Maybe the next one is the one I've always been looking for.'

Another bell, this time at the back door. Before I can get there, it rings again.

'It's The Milkman,' the customer at the counter says, without turning around. 'He always rings twice.'

Davy starts to cry. His pacifier drops out of his mouth, hits the floor and starts to roll.

Jerome is there now, and his camera follows the pacifier across the floor, past LaRoche's vacant, pale eyes. It comes to a stop in front of a pair of European loafers.

The camera pans up. Lean thighs. Narrow waist. Sculpted biceps. Dark Italian eyes. Antonio.

Janalee sighs and sets Davy down. Still wailing, he crawls across the floor toward his pacifier. Antonio leans down and gives it to him. Davy smiles at him and begins to play soldiers on his father's bloodied head.

'Davy wants to play with his daddy,' Amy says plaintively. She's crying, too, and holding a cellphone.

'He's playing *on* his daddy,' I point out.

Davy begins to giggle, and giggle, and giggle …

I WAS BOLT UPRIGHT in bed.

My radio alarm was on, and the remnants of Davy's maniacal giggling had morphed into the happy talk of the local morning team. I wasn't sure which was worse. In response to my movement, Frank jumped up on the bed. For once, I didn't try to push him off.

Instead, I settled back on to the pillow and scratched his head, which he had accommodatingly plopped onto my stomach. It was obvious the dream had been sparked by my viewing of *The Postman Always Rings Twice* last night. Instead of the black and white of the original 1946 noir classic, though, the dream had been in vivid color. So vivid that it had almost hurt to watch it. The details, the colors—all overwhelming.

I had been able to see individual tears run down Davy's face, practically count Antonio's eyelashes. The three earrings in Amy's left ear were all pink gold. One of them had a tiny turquoise stone. Janalee had been wearing blue eyeshadow and her mascara was smudged. La Roche's already pale blue eyes were starting to cloud over, like a bad case of post-mortem cataracts.

Wait a second. I rewound the scene in my mind. Janalee's tears. LaRoche's staring eyes. Janalee had—both in the dream and in real life—blue eyes. LaRoche, the same. But Davy...

I thought about the times I'd seen the baby. Davy's eyes were brown, I was certain of that. Could two blue-eyed parents have a brown-eyed baby?

'No!' I said, with all the conviction a single biology class could give you. But I also knew that Davy wasn't adopted, because I'd seen Janalee pregnant. Could his birth have been the result of *in vitro* fertilization? A possibility, of course.

But Davy's dark eyes were very much like the eyes of someone else I knew, and while the surrealistic quality of the dream might have magnified the resemblance, it certainly hadn't manufactured it.

'That's why I keep feeling like Davy has adult eyes,' I said. 'Because I've *seen* them in an adult.'

When Frank didn't respond, I gently knock-knocked on the top of his head. He raised it.

'Guess what?' I asked, moving aside a lock of hair so I could see his still closed eyes.

Frank yawned and opened one of them.

'Davy,' I said triumphantly, 'looks like The Milkman.'

TWENTY

'THE MORE I THOUGHT about it, the more sense it made,' I told Sarah in the exhibit hall later that morning.

She was busy trying to keep the exhibitors from breaking down their booths early. It being Sunday and the last day of the convention, the crowd was light. Those who weren't in their hotel rooms packing to leave were either at the cupping or the frothing exhibition.

Nonetheless, the exhibit hall was billed as being open until noon, and it wasn't going to close early under Sarah's watch, come hell or homicide.

'Antonio has brown eyes,' I continued, as I trailed after her. 'And Davy has brown eyes. Davy is also colicky. A milk allergy perhaps?' I raised my eyebrows at Sarah.

'You *do* remember I never had kids, right? That I inherited the two that live with me?'

Oh, yeah. 'A milk allergy can contribute to colic and Antonio told me just this week that he can't drink dairy.'

'The *Milkman* doesn't drink milk?' Sarah asked.

'Weird, huh?' I said. 'But maybe it makes it easier. You know, like candy-makers who don't eat chocolate. They don't have to worry about being tempted to eat the profits.'

'I doubt that two-percent and skim have exactly the siren call of truffles and peanut butter cups,' Sarah said dryly. She started after a booth-holder who was surreptitiously sliding a cardboard packing box out from under his table.

When he saw her, he raised his hands in surrender and kicked the box back under the table. Sarah backed off.

'According to my biology class,' I continued, uncowed, 'lactose intolerance is quite common amongst people of middle European and Mediterranean descent.'

'God knows I don't want to badmouth your biology teacher from the ninth grade,' Sarah said, checking her clipboard, 'but I don't think either the "blue or brown", "burp or don't burp" thing is scientific proof.'

'Perhaps not,' I said. 'I did a little Internet research this morning and I did find some…caveats.'

She looked sideways at me. 'Like what kind of caveats?'

'They say it's "rare" for two blue-eyed parents to have a brown-eyed child. Rare,' I repeated disgustedly. 'Whatever happened to downright impossible?'

Sarah patted me on the shoulder. 'I think I speak for the rest of the free world when I say I'm sorry we all can't be as black-and-white as you are.'

'Apology accepted,' I said, sadly shaking my head. 'But where does this leave us?'

'Leave *us?*' she asked. 'It leaves me patrolling these yahoos until noon. Then it leaves me making sure they use union workers to transport their stuff, or all hell is going to break loose.' She took a hit of her puffer. 'Who knew that coffee vendors were such loose cannons?'

'Hey, speaking of loose cannons,' I said, glancing around, 'have you seen Levitt this morning?'

'I did,' Sarah said, 'and he's looking a little banged up. Apparently, black and blue is the new green.'

'Poor Levitt. I should probably check on him to make sure he's all right.'

Sarah snorted. 'Don't give me that. You're just feeling guilty because you were glad he fell over.'

'I was not glad.' Relieved maybe, but not glad.

'Right.' Sarah didn't look convinced, but since she was busy patrolling for vendors trying to make a break for it, she let me off the hook. 'The last I saw of Levitt, Penny was trying to get him to sign a release so he wouldn't sue the joint.'

'What in the world got into him, do you suppose?' I asked.

'I'd say nearly a bottle of wine,' Sarah said dryly.

Given my friend's mood this morning, I didn't bother to ask what had gotten into her to offer the obviously inebriated Levitt the stage and an open mic. Asking Sarah to explain herself was like asking the wind why it blew dirt in your eyes. It just did.

'True,' I said, instead. 'I know he drank it down fast, but should a man his size get falling-down drunk on three glasses of wine?'

'Maybe he's not as used to it as you are.'

I ignored the besmirching of my character. 'He did turn the wine down, the first time around,' I said, more to myself than to her. 'It was only when Pavlik started questioning him that he began to drink.'

'While we're on the subject of Pavlik, did you get any last night?' Sarah showed her teeth.

'No,' I said shortly.

Pavlik's game with the phantom camera in the corridor wasn't sitting well with me. What did he think I was going to do? Break down and confess? I didn't think so. He hadn't seemed to take me seriously as a suspect. I did think, though, that he took me seriously as an informant.

My best guess was that he wanted to squeeze as much information as he could from me. And he sure knew how to do it. I had volunteered far more than I would have, if I hadn't thought he had me on tape. Despite my attraction to him, Pavlik still made me a little nervous.

Sarah and I had lapped the floor three times now. She stopped at the door. 'Touched a nerve, did I?'

'No, you did not,' I grumbled. 'And it's crass of you to ask anyway.'

'I just know the benefits of having a professional check under your hood,' she said. The dirty grin on her face told me that *she,* at least, had 'gotten some' last night.

'And you have the nerve to call the trophy "Slut in a cup",' I said, and Sarah's grin got even bigger. 'The engineer, I presume?'

'Mike,' she supplied. 'Who, by the way, apologized for turning on Levitt's mic at just the right—or wrong—time.'

I shook my head. 'Who knew that someone who looks like a preacher could have a mouth like that?'

'He came up with body parts, and things to do with them, that even I have never thought of.'

That was hard to believe. 'Well, at least we had a mature audience,' I said.

Sarah shrugged. 'Too bad about the Taylor wedding down the hall, though.'

'The wedding?' I asked. 'You mean the wedding that was getting our audio feed until your Mike fixed it?'

'Yeah, the fix didn't quite take. Mike's sorry about that, too.' Sarah didn't look like she was sorry for much of anything. 'You might want to stay away from Penny for the rest of Java Ho. She's not in a very jolly mood.'

'It wasn't my fault their sound system got its wires crossed,' I pointed out.

'True, but they seem to frown on public obscenity,' Sarah said. 'As does the father of the bride. And the flower girl.'

This could be a very long day. 'None of this is my fault,' I whined. I went to look at my watch, and then realized I must have left it on my dresser. Instead, I pulled out my cellphone to check the time.

'Nine fifteen. I'm going to look for Levitt and Amy.' I was hoping I could find out more about the relationship between the two of them. And the relationship between Antonio and Janalee. And God knew who else in this place.

'I saw Amy about half an hour ago, with Janalee,' Sarah said. As I started to turn away, she added, 'Oh, and that camera kid was looking for you, too.'

Jerome. I hadn't gotten a chance to talk to him last night, but I knew he had been shooting tape and probably had some prime footage from last night. Footage more suited to X-roll, than B-roll. I'd have to track him down to see what he and Kate planned to do with it.

I thanked Sarah and headed for the Grand Foyer. As I rounded the corner, I saw Penny. An older man was on her heels, apparently haranguing her. Definite father-of-the-bride material. I ducked behind a pillar.

'Of all the pillars in all the world,' Levitt intoned.

I turned. 'You look awful.'

And he did. Even though Levitt had toppled over backwards, he'd tried to break his fall by twisting sideways. It had probably kept him from bashing the back of his skull into the floor, but he'd hit his nose on Amy's chair on the way down.

'Is it broken?' I asked, feeling terrible.

He felt his bandaged nose gingerly. Both eyes were black. 'It is, and it serves me right, I fear. I'm so sorry for ruining your banquet, Maggy. If that weren't bad enough, I also squandered the opportunity you afforded me to spread the word about EarthBean and further our cause.'

He shook his head dejectedly. 'The only saving grace is that I didn't get on that podium. I have no idea what I might have said.'

I sighed. There was something about Levitt that made me want to head to the confessional. And I wasn't even Catholic. 'I hate to admit it, but when you fell over before you could get up there...' I trailed off.

'You were relieved,' Levitt supplied quietly. 'Don't be ashamed, Maggy. The fall hurt physically, it's true, but the nose will heal, and the headache will dissipate. I'm not sure I would ever have recovered from making a fool of myself publicly.' He grimaced. 'Even *more* publicly.'

I touched his hand. 'Levitt, forgive me, but what happened last night seemed completely out of character for you.'

'It is—for the me you know.' He looked like he was going to cry. 'But it's not out of character, I'm sorry to say, for the person I used to be. That's why I'm so terribly ashamed.'

'You're an alcoholic,' I hazarded. 'That's why you didn't order wine in the first place.'

He nodded. 'I cannot handle alcohol. I never could, but back then I kept trying.' He gave me a little self-conscious smile. 'When the sheriff starting questioning me, I just caved in. There was nothing even Amy could do about it.'

'Amy?' I just let it hang there.

'I know people talk about us,' Levitt said, 'but Amy is my AA sponsor.'

So that would mean that Amy was a recovering alcoholic as well. She seemed terribly young to have been through all that, but Eric had friends who seemed well on the road to addiction in high school. Even younger. 'The argument you had with LaRoche?'

Levitt cracked a grin. 'The one *before* his speech or the one afterwards?'

'Before,' I said, with an answering smile. 'George said…I mean, I've been told LaRoche seemed to be telling you to stay away from Amy. Didn't he know she was your sponsor?'

'No,' Levitt said. 'We are supposed to keep those things private.'

'Of course. That would be the "anonymous" part, wouldn't it?'

'It would,' Levitt conceded kindly. 'But even beyond that, I didn't think it was any of LaRoche's business.'

'But then what was LaRoche's beef with you? As you say, what business of his was it, even if he did think you and Amy were having an affair?'

Levitt shifted uncomfortably. 'Quite honestly, his reaction took me completely by surprise. I don't know what was behind it.'

'And now we never will know,' I said, thinking that Amy might be the only one who did. I stuck my head around the pillar. 'Looks like we're safe. Penny and the father of the bride are gone.'

'Again, Maggy,' Levitt said, stepping out from behind the pillar, 'please accept my apologies.' He stuck out his hand.

I took it. 'Apology accepted. Assuming you're back at meetings.'

'I am. That's where Amy took me last night. I have to say, it wasn't where I wanted to go. But it was where I needed to be.'

'I'm glad,' I said. I was thinking how simple—and profound—that was. If only we all were that clear about where that place was. I was about to turn away, when I stopped. 'Levitt?'

He looked up.

'If you didn't tell LaRoche, why did you tell me?'

'*You,* I like.' He smiled and walked away.

I HAD FOUND LEVITT when I was avoiding Penny. Now I found Jerome as I was avoiding Pavlik. The sheriff was striding toward the exhibit hall looking self-important. And handsome. I hated that.

But whether he was handsome or not, I wasn't ready to talk to him after last night. Maybe I was punishing him for tricking me. More likely, I was punishing myself for being so gullible. I ducked into the snack bar, where I found Jerome sitting at a table and eating French fries.

'Fast food before ten?' I commented, taking the seat across from him. The 'mom' gene dies hard.

Jerome held up a fry for my inspection. 'A perfectly fried potato should be enjoyed at any time.' He rotated the fry. 'Look at it: an impudent little fry, golden brown, perfectly salted, served at its peak.'

'No ketchup?'

He gasped. 'Please. Would you put ketchup on lobster?'

'Actually, I did once,' I admitted. 'A long time ago, before I knew it was *supposed* to taste like that.' I waved my gastronomical shortcomings away. 'Listen, I saw you last night, but didn't get a chance to talk to you. Is everything all right?'

'Sure.' Jerome was applying himself to the fries. 'Some night, huh?'

'Yup.'

When I didn't say more, Jerome sat back in his chair. 'You're wondering what I'm going to do with the tape.' It was a statement, not a question.

'I am.' I hooked a fry. 'I know you're a journalist and have a responsibility both to your profession and to Kate, but I'd really hate to see people embarrassed.'

Jerome grabbed back his fry. 'Laying it on a little thick, aren't you?'

'Is it working?'

He shook his head. 'No more than ketchup does on lobster.'

'Actually,' I said, grabbing another fry. 'That wasn't half bad. Same principle as cocktail sauce on shrimp.'

'I suppose.' He was quiet for second, then: 'Listen, I'm the one who accidentally blew the whistle on you. That's why I was avoiding you last night.'

'You were avoiding me?' Nice of me to notice.

Jerome squirmed. 'I figure we're friends.' He lowered his voice. 'The last thing I meant to do was implicate you in a murder.'

Of course. Pavlik had known that I was in the competition room the night of LaRoche's murder. It's the only reason he would have bothered with his little deception about the nonexistent camera. Someone must have told him. If I'd given it any thought, I would have pegged Kate as the whistleblower, thinking she'd seen me head that direction from the bar.

Now I realized Jerome could have seen me, too. Poor kid—probably thought I was going to the slammer. Couldn't blame him for thinking that, though. I'd been of the same mind.

I was about to tell him that the timeline had cleared me, when Jerome ducked—his head nearly on the table. 'It's the sheriff,' he hissed. 'And he's coming this way.'

Sure enough, Pavlik was enroute with a soft drink in his hand.

'Maybe he's just looking for a place to sit,' Jerome whispered hopefully.

'Doubt it,' I said, looking around. Except for us, the place was deserted. Snack bars that serve hot dogs, hamburgers, fries and hot pretzels, aren't exactly break-fast hot spots. 'But don't worry, it will be all right.' I patted his hand.

Jerome stood up abruptly. 'You run, I'll divert him.'

I stayed where I was. 'Really, Jerome, it's fine.'

'Excuse me.' The sheriff was in town. 'I don't mean to interrupt, but I need to talk to you, Ms Thorsen.' He looked pointedly at Jerome. 'Alone.'

I thought Jerome's eyes were going to bug out of his head. 'All right, well, then. I guess I'll go…um…see you later, Maggy.' He ran out of the snack bar.

Pavlik watched him go. 'Should we be worried about that kid?'

'No,' I said. 'He just thinks you're going to arrest me for murder.'

'And you're so sure I'm not?' Pavlik grabbed a fry from the box Jerome had left. 'Cold.' He tossed it back.

'I figure you would have arrested me already, if you were going to. And besides—' my eyes narrowed—'your little trick last night got you all the information you wanted.'

Pavlik laughed, and his eyes went all blue and sparkly. 'Sorry, but you're so easy. I couldn't help myself.'

Apparently not so easy that he *did* help himself. At least I was no 'Slut in a cup'.

'Sarah said something similar the last time she tortured me,' I said. 'Glad I can bring you both such pleasure.'

He took my hand and turned it over, rubbing his thumb gently across the palm. 'I plan to bring you even more pleasure, as soon as we both have time.'

'Whe…' I squeaked and had to clear my throat. 'When might that be?'

'As soon as I close this case,' he said, taking out the damn notepad. 'So what do you have for me?'

'What do I have for you?' I repeated, with the proper pronoun changes. 'Maybe it's time you shared a little information with me.'

'Fair enough,' he said agreeably as he thumbed through his notes. 'Let's see. How about the fact that Levitt Fredericks has an alibi? A questionable one, maybe, but an alibi nonetheless.'

'What is it?' I asked. Yesterday I would have thrown Levitt to the dogs to save myself. In fact, I had done just that. Now I only wanted to save him.

'Your barista, Amy. She says they were together.'

'She's not my barista,' I protested. 'And why do you say Levitt's alibi is questionable? You think Amy is lying?'

Pavlik rubbed his chin, which had a fine bit of stubble on it. And a mighty fine bit of stubble it was. 'Your bartender was right—they're romantically involved. If she loves him, she could be lying to give him an alibi.'

'He's not my bartender,' I automatically corrected. 'And Amy wouldn't do that.'

I was thinking furiously. Levitt hadn't told the sheriff that Amy was his AA sponsor. Since he hadn't chosen to share that information, I certainly couldn't.

Or shouldn't. And probably wouldn't.

'You didn't even know that she and Fredericks were an item,' Pavlik was saying. 'How well do you really know her?'

Truth was, I didn't know Amy very well at all. In fact, before Caron had targeted her as a barista acquisition, Amy and I were casual smile-and-wave kind of acquaintances, at most.

Still, Levitt had entrusted me with some very personal information, about both him and Amy. I couldn't betray that trust, but I also couldn't let Pavlik go off in the wrong direction.

In other words, I couldn't just shut up.

'Listen,' I said, 'I can't tell you why, but I'm almost certain that Amy is telling the truth.'

Pavlik squinted. 'And why am I supposed to take that as gospel?'

'You're *supposed* to believe in me. That's what the cop–slash–love interest does.'

'Is that what I am?' Pavlik asked. 'The cop–slash–love interest?' That glint in his eye was back again.

'You would be if we ever had a moment to spend together. A date, even,' I said irritably. 'But for now you just have to have faith in me.'

'Even though you don't have enough in me to tell me what you know?' he shot back.

'That's not fair,' I protested. 'I would tell you if I could.'

Pavlik stood up and tossed his untouched drink cup into the trash bin nearby. '*Now* do you understand why I told you there was a camera in that back hallway?'

'No,' I said, standing up, too. 'I don't.'

He touched my forehead gently, almost sadly. 'You have all this information running around in your head, but you try to filter it. You know all these people—their comings and goings, their secrets. And you want to protect them.'

'Just the good ones,' I said softly.

'Problem is, we don't know which ones are the good guys, and which ones are the bad. I can help you figure that out, if you'll trust me.' He cupped my chin.

I was already teary-eyed and I started to feel that crushing heaviness that takes your breath away. 'But if I tell you things in the wrong way, if I use the wrong words—' I was having trouble getting any words out now— 'you could arrest someone who is innocent.'

I wasn't explaining this very well. I tried again. 'It's like in the doctor's office. You say you have an earache and, before you finish talking, the doctor is writing out a prescription for an ear infection. He stops listening when he hears what he wants to hear.'

'You're saying I jump to conclusions?' His eyes were stormy now.

'No, no.' I tried to take his hand, but he still held the notepad in it. 'You play the percentages, Pavlik. And I understand that you have to.'

'The percentage bets are usually right,' he pointed out. 'That's why they're percentage bets.'

'I know that,' I said. 'And ninety-five percent of the time it is an ear infection. I just don't want to be responsible for giving you the wrong information—the information that makes you stop listening.

'I say affair, you suspect one person. Illegitimate child, another. Money troubles, another. It's so easy to make judgments when you're on the outside look-ing in. Things are not that simple. Life is just not that simple.'

Now I shut my mouth.

Too late. A vein was pulsing in Pavlik's forehead. He started to say something and then stopped. He started to walk away and stopped that, too.

He turned back.

'So, who's the illegitimate kid?'

TWENTY-ONE

OK, SO I CAVED. SHOOT ME.

I told Pavlik everything.

Well, almost everything. The one thing I didn't tell him was that Levitt and Amy were recovering—or in Levitt's case, semi-recovering—alcoholics. I felt that Levitt had told me in confidence, and I wouldn't break that. Not even for Pavlik.

But given that Davy was the only kid in the cast of characters, it hadn't taken Pavlik a nanosecond to deduce he was the illegitimate one. Once that particular bean was spilled, I figured the more information I could give Pavlik the better. I'd haul in all the trees, and let him decide if they constituted a forest.

For the record, Pavlik didn't quite buy the blue eye/brown eye thing. And the lactose intolerant part he just laughed at.

'I don't think gassy is one of the markers on a paternity test,' he said.

'I think you're taking lactose intolerance a little too lightly, Sheriff,' I said. 'It can be debilitating.'

'I'll take your word for it.'

I ignored that. 'Also, LaRoche was cross-eyed, which can be inherited. Davy is not.'

'I think it depends on the cause,' Pavlik said.

Details, details. 'Well, eyes and intestinal distur-
bances aside, I'm willing to bet you'll see the resemblance if you look for it.'

We were standing in the corner of the Grand Foyer
nearest the door to the exhibit hall. I was hoping that
Janalee would come in with Davy.

And stand next to Antonio.

And a little psychedelic lighting, like in my dream,
couldn't hurt, either.

'Even if you're right,' Pavlik was saying, 'maybe La-
Roche was shooting blanks, and he and Janalee used a
sperm donor.'

'Possible,' I admitted. 'But don't you want to know
for sure? If Antonio and Janalee had an affair, it opens
a lot of possibilities.'

'For the sake of argument,' Pavlik said, leaning back
against the wall, 'if they had an affair and if Davy is
Antonio's baby, don't you think LaRoche would have
noticed the kid didn't look like him?'

'Please. LaRoche was so supremely self-centered, the
only time he noticed Davy was when he played with his
soldiers.'

As I spoke, I saw Sarah leave the exhibit hall at a
full run. She went out the front revolving door, leaving
it spinning in her wake.

'Should I ask what "his soldiers" are?' Pavlik said.
'I think it might be indictable.'

I laughed, wondering what was up with Sarah's abrupt
departure. 'LaRoche is…was a military buff. He has toy
soldiers all over his office.'

Pavlik might have found my lactose intolerance theory
lacking, but now he looked fascinated. 'Toy soldiers?
The lead ones? Those things are great.'

'They looked like metal of some kind,' I said hesitantly. I hadn't touched the ones in LaRoche's office, so I couldn't be sure. 'But why would they make a toy out of lead?'

'These aren't for kids.' Pavlik looked astonished at the thought. Toys? For children?

'Some are antiques,' he continued, 'and others are made as new collectibles.'

'That explains why LaRoche grabbed it away from Davy,' I said, thinking back.

'Damn right,' Pavlik said vehemently. 'Those things are worth a fortune.'

Guys really were a different species. 'I meant that he took the soldier away to keep Davy safe from the lead.'

'Which, if it's true,' Pavlik said, pushing off from the wall, 'proves my point. LaRoche obviously cares about the kid. *His* kid. So, are we done here?'

But I'd been thinking something over. LaRoche was, after all, a man, and an unusually self-important one. 'You know, you may have been right the first time.'

'Of course I am,' Pavlik said, brushing a strand of hair away from my eyes. 'It's common knowledge that a guy has a right to protect his little soldiers.'

'With a little soldiers cup, no doubt,' I said with a grin.

'Nicely put.' Pavlik looked around and, seeing no one paying attention, gave me a kiss on the nose. 'Much as I would like to continue this conversation, I need to go. Try not to get into trouble.'

'First, you want me involved,' I pointed out. 'Then you don't.'

'I think I've extracted all the information I can from you,' he said with a smile.

Then he got serious. 'One thing you might want to give some thought to: if you're right about Davy—' he held up his hands— 'and I'm not saying that you are, why would this all hit the fan now? Why did someone need to kill LaRoche *now?*'

Pavlik was right, I thought as I watched him walk away. Something had precipitated the murder of La-Roche. But what?

As I stayed in the corner cogitating, people milled around in the entry hall. With the cupping and frothing events over, there was nothing left to do but say goodbye. People would go home and Java Ho would disappear, only to rise again at this time next year.

A sort of caffeinated Brigadoon, one where—as Pavlik put it—something had hit the fan. And then LaRoche.

But why now? And why here?

The fire at Janalee's Place was the most earth-shaking of the events immediately surrounding Java Ho. La-Roche had accused me of both starting it and trying to steal Amy.

LaRoche was also worried about Levitt stealing Amy in a very different way. Davy's parentage could be a factor, too, if LaRoche had just found out about it. Had he? If so, how?

LaRoche and Antonio were arguing just before La-Roche and I had done likewise. Levitt and LaRoche had their shouting match after that. And another one the day before.

LaRoche should have had 'Please take a number' stamped on his forehead. Was there anyone he didn't tick off?

Knowing what I knew now about Levitt's alibi and Davy's questionable parentage, Antonio's argument seemed the most pertinent. Had he told LaRoche that Davy was his—Antonio's—baby? If so, why? Or, as Pavlik would say, why now?

I remembered the tears in LaRoche's eyes when I came up to him that night. They had seemed out of character, but maybe the guy had more sensitivity than I gave him credit for. Then again, Fall was ragweed season. Maybe LaRoche simply had hay fever.

Sad or stuffy, though, shouldn't LaRoche have been the one who wanted to kill Antonio, not the other way around? Unless, of course, Antonio had killed LaRoche in self-defense.

As with my theory about Levitt in the same scenario, Antonio might have to go to jail, but probably not for too terribly long. It had been an accident, after all. I tried not to think about the fact that if I was right, Antonio also had left LaRoche under the trophy table to die.

Why was nothing clear cut?

Still seeing no sign of Janalee or Antonio, I left my post in the corner and entered the exhibit hall.

I'D NEVER SEEN so much corrugated cardboard.

Apparently taking advantage of Sarah's absence, the vendors were packing up with a vengeance. Espresso machines, still steaming, jammed into boxes. Coffee beans flying through the air. A smoothie machine running amuck in shrink-wrap.

Had the coffee world gone mad? I checked the time. Quarter to twelve.

'Stop!'

It was like watching a giant game of statue-maker. Everyone froze in their place. Even the coffee beans would have stayed in mid-air if they knew what was good for them.

Sarah was back. She strode down the center aisle, the smell of cigarette smoke wafting behind her. She was tapping her watch. 'You people,' she announced, 'have a contractual agreement to be here until noon.'

'It doesn't say anything about having to be *in* the booth,' a voice said.

A laugh from the crowd, immediately stifled.

'Who said that?' Sarah demanded. 'Speak up!'

I only hoped she wouldn't start shooting the vendors one by one until someone gave up a name.

A hand was raised shakily. Sucker.

Much as I wanted to stay and watch the execution, I had caught sight of Antonio on the far side of the hall. He was wearing a suit and tie, like he'd just come from church. It was Sunday, I reminded myself.

I hailed him, and he waited for me to catch up.

'Good morning, Maggy,' he said, as we walked together. 'Are you very glad to have the convention behind you?'

'I am,' I admitted, 'though I'm afraid Sarah will have all the exhibitors stay after.'

'Stay after what?'

Me and my idioms. 'Sorry, I meant as a punishment, like staying after school.'

'Ahh.' He nodded in understanding. 'I like your friend, Sarah. She says what she's thinking and that's unusual.' He stopped and looked at me. 'Most times you are that way, too.'

'I hope so,' I said, not knowing quite what to say.

Antonio just waited. And waited.

'You want me to say what I'm thinking?' I ventured.

'I do,' he said. 'I think you have something that is on your mind.'

He was being so civilized about it, that I was feeling guilty about suspecting him. Even if I wanted to interrogate him, where does one properly start? Murder or adultery?

'I told you I saw your argument with LaRoche the night of the murder.'

'Yes,' Antonio said. The only indication that he was feeling angry, or fearful, or anything at all, was the slightest tightening of his mouth. 'And I believe that you, too, argued with him, Maggy. After.'

'True,' I admitted. 'I wanted LaRoche to recuse himself as a judge because Amy and Janalee were finalists in the barista competition.'

'And he refused?'

'He did.'

'I am not surprised,' Antonio said. 'I believe he very much wanted HotWired to win.'

'Do you believe he would have cheated to achieve that?' I was falling into Antonio's more formal way of speaking.

He shrugged. 'Who says what a man will do?'

Not me, that was for sure. While I'd felt recusing himself was the right thing for LaRoche to do, I had been worried about the perception of favoritism, not outright fraud.

'But if he did cheat,' Antonio was saying, 'it would be for his business, for money. Not for Janalee or for Amy.'

'But he cared enough about Amy to be upset at the thought of her seeing Levitt.'

Antonio seemed surprised at that. 'He said this?'

'He said he wanted Levitt to leave Amy alone.' I was watching Antonio carefully for his reaction.

'Amy was with Levitt because of the drink.' So Antonio knew about AA somehow. 'They were friends, though many people assume that a man and a woman cannot simply be friends.'

When Harry Met Sally. 'Why would LaRoche care what their relationship was?'

'Marvin LaRoche cared about his property.' Antonio said it quietly.

'And Amy was his property?' I hazarded, still trying to skewer the heart of the matter.

The Milkman pulled at his tie. 'I have said too much.'

'Listen, Antonio,' I persisted. 'LaRoche accused me of burning down Janalee's Place to lure Amy away. He seemed more concerned about losing her than the store.' I said this last part slowly, because it hadn't occurred to me before. 'Why?'

'Janalee's Place was never LaRoche's property,' he said. 'It was Janalee's.'

Before I could ask anything else, Antonio straightened his tie. 'I must go now, Maggy, and help my employees pack up. It was very good to see you.' He strode away from me.

'And what about Davy?' I called after him. 'Was Davy his property, too?'

Antonio stopped dead. When he finally turned, his face was composed, resolute.

'No, Maggy. David was not.'

TWENTY-TWO

As I TRIED TO DIGEST what Antonio had just told me and decipher what he hadn't, a piercing whistle sounded from inside the exhibit hall.

Once, twice, three times. Each one louder and shriller than the preceding. The last was followed by the sound of stampeding feet, screeching cardboard and squeaking carts.

I pulled out my cellphone to check the time. Sure enough, noon on the dot. The exhibitors had been freed.

Sarah came out, looking fried.

'You didn't hurt anybody in there, did you?' I asked.

'I threatened one guy with a paper cut,' she said. 'That's about it.'

'Regular paper or cardboard?'

'Corrugated cardboard. But he deserved it.' She shook her head. 'I don't know what I was thinking when I took this on. These people make homebuyers look good.'

'I told you so.'

Sarah threw me a look that had paper cut written all over it.

'Besides, you're a real estate agent,' I said reasonably. 'Homebuyers are your customers. Aren't you supposed to like them?'

'Yeah, and you like yours, I suppose.'

'Of course I do.' Some days. And for short bursts of time.

'I'm going out for a smoke.'

'You quit.'

'I'm down to smoking by proxy. Leave me alone.' And with that she stomped off.

'Wait,' I called after her. 'Shouldn't someone keep tabs on the—'

I was interrupted by a crash from the exhibit hall. Sarah's reaction was to break into a run. Toward the revolving door.

I stifled a groan. Unlike Sarah, I'd had no real responsibilities today. I deserved to be punished.

As I stuffed my cellphone back into my purse in preparation for investigating the crash, it triggered a memory. Amy had been talking on a cellphone when I'd seen her sitting in her SUV outside the grocery store. She had been crying.

Antonio had said LaRoche considered Amy his property. I had a hunch he was talking personal property, not business. I figured Antonio thought—or knew—that Amy and LaRoche were having an affair, but was too much of a gentleman to say it.

So, was Amy talking to LaRoche on the phone? Possibly. Or to Levitt on the verge of a setback? Even more likely. There was no way of knowing short of asking Amy. If it hadn't been the night of the fire, I wouldn't be giving the incident a second thought.

But it *had* been the night of the fire. Amy said she'd gone back to drop off her purchases that night. In the process of doing that, she had discovered the fire and been burned. Now I had to wonder whether she'd known the place was about to be torched and had gone back to either stop it or to salvage something.

Then again, maybe she'd set the fire herself.

When we'd spoken at Schultz's Market, Amy was unloading her basket. As I recalled, though, it contained nothing but some kitchen utensils. So, what had I been expecting? A can of lighter fluid? Matches?

Well, yes. But as I told Pavlik, nothing in life was that simple. Still, Amy could have picked up the tools of the arson trade after I left. As I recalled, the lighter fluid and charcoal were along the wall by the checkouts.

So, where was I?

Amy was crying. And she could have burned down Janalee's Place.

Antonio was almost undoubtedly Davy's father. Which made him Janalee's lover.

LaRoche had been jealous of Levitt. And may have been having an affair with Amy.

This wasn't a love triangle, it was a hexagon.

Lost in thought, I stumbled over a cable.

A hand steadied me. 'I'm sorry, Maggy,' Jerome said.

'For which? Leaving me with the sheriff in the snack bar or nearly breaking my ankle?' I was exaggerating on both counts, but I was hoping to make him feel guilty. Then I selfishly could bend him to my purposes. I was a bad, bad woman.

'Both,' he said sheepishly. 'What did the sheriff say?'

'He questioned me,' I said. I left out the kissing part.

Jerome flushed. 'Believe me, Maggy. If there's anything I can do…?'

Bingo. 'In fact, there is.'

'Anything.' He looked so earnest, I was almost ashamed.

'You can tell me what you and Kate are planning to do with the tape you're shooting.'

My reasons for wanting to know were twofold: first, I wanted to make sure Levitt wasn't publicly embarrassed or privately blackmailed by what was taped the night of the banquet. Second, if Kate was going to make money on this, I wanted my cut. But only assuming the former didn't happen. I did have my ethics, after all. I drew the line at making money on the humiliation of a friend.

'Kate and I are putting together a pitch for a new reality show.' He held up a hand like he was delineating a marquee. 'You know, real-life people, trapped at a convention with only caffeine, a hot dog stand and a bar. How long before they break?'

I would break Kate, the weasel. She was doing a tacky, derivative version of what I had wanted to do. But now couldn't. Because *I* had ethics. And friends.

I sighed. 'Don't you need releases?'

'Yeah.' He pulled a sheaf of papers out of his jeans pocket. 'I couldn't believe how eager people are to be on TV.'

And to be made fools of. 'Please tell me Levitt Fredericks didn't sign one of those.'

Jerome shook his head. 'No, he was the one hold-out. Kate's working on him.'

I didn't think Levitt would give in, but I also didn't trust Kate.

'You said you would do anything for me, right?' I asked Jerome.

'Of course.'

'Destroy the section of the tape that shows Levitt falling over.' Release or not, I was afraid the tape would get out somehow. Maybe plastered on the Internet.

'But that's the centerpiece of the program,' Jerome protested. 'Kate would—'

I pulled him aside to make sure we weren't overheard. 'Jerome, I have a feeling you've been faced with some major issues already in your life. Issues that have made you very mature at a young age.'

He squirmed and I held up my hand. 'I'm not asking. It's not my place. The only reason I brought it up is that Levitt has faced some problems, too, admittedly of his own making. But he had worked his way through them. Until Saturday night.'

Jerome got it. 'A relapse, of sorts.'

'Of sorts.'

He rubbed the top of his head. Then he seemed to come to a decision.

'Kate is going to kill me,' he announced loudly.

'Oh?' I asked.

'Yeah, I accidentally deleted about thirty seconds of tape.' He grinned. 'Don't know how it happened.'

'I do,' I said, touching his shoulder. 'An honorable man, doing the right thing. Thank you.'

'No. Thank you, Maggy.' He suddenly looked ten years older than his age, rather than ten years younger. 'I appreciate that you recognized something in me, but

I also appreciate you not asking a lot of questions.' He shrugged. 'Cancer is not a place I like to visit unless I have to.'

'Understood.' I stuck out my hand. 'It's been a pleasure working with you.'

'Same here,' he said, shaking my hand. 'I hope we'll have the opportunity to do it again.'

'Me, too.' I turned away, tears burning at the corners of my eyes. His words shouldn't have more meaning than the same ones spoken by any other twenty-one-year-old. But they did.

Blinking, I looked around for the source of the earlier crash. Nothing. In fact, all of Java Ho had seemed to fold its tent and silently—or not so silently—steal away. In its place, the national association of roofers was waiting in the wings to move in. Signs welcoming their members already were stacked up along one wall.

The end of a convention, especially one you've been an integral part of, is a little sad and a lot weird.

With the exception of the unfortunate Taylor wedding, Java Ho had owned the convention center. Now all our people were leaving or already gone, and strangers were moving in.

It felt weird, but not so sad. I didn't mind leaving Java Ho—and Marvin LaRoche—behind this time.

I wandered into what had been the competition room. Even this, the crime scene, was cleared out. No stage, no trophy table, no body. Not even the oval-shaped stain that had started it all—at least my part of it. Just a plain blue carpet waiting for the next row of chairs, the next trample of feet.

A scratch at the door and I turned. Janalee was peeking in with Davy. They came in quietly. 'It feels so odd, so hushed,' Janalee said. 'Like church.'

Janalee looked like she had just come from there. She was wearing a black long-sleeved, high-necked dress, not unlike the one I'd worn to the banquet, but without the no-shoulder look. At Janalee's words, Davy started to whimper.

'Though it's the crying room we see mostly at church these days,' she admitted with a sad smile. 'Davy's been sick a lot lately.'

'I'm sorry,' I said, and I meant it. I'd just assumed Davy was a particularly unpleasant baby, to be honest. I hoped Janalee wasn't dealing with both a dead husband and a truly ill baby. 'Is it anything serious?'

Janalee gave up trying to placate Davy and set him down on the floor. The baby crawled a few feet away and sat, sucking his thumb. It reminded me of my dream and I had to restrain a shiver.

'Davy has dangerous levels of lead in his system,' Janalee said simply.

I gave a start. 'From LaRoche's…um, I mean, Marvin's soldiers?'

'Yes.' She sighed. 'Marvin tried to blame it on Janalee's Place. He said there must have been lead in the paint there.'

'There wasn't?' I asked.

'Not for years,' she said. 'Marvin was just trying to blame Davy's illness on me.'

She shrugged. 'But that was Marvin. Taking credit for the good things and looking for someone to blame for the bad.'

'But how did Davy get hold of the soldiers?' I was remembering how LaRoche had snatched the toy away from Davy in his office.

'When Davy was younger,' Janalee said. 'I would leave him with Marvin. He would give him an old soldier to play with. Not one of his good ones, of course. God forbid Davy would lower its value.'

She shrugged. 'But Davy was teething.'

'And teething babies put things in their mouths,' I said.

'Babies put *every*thing in their mouths,' Janalee said. 'I told Marvin that. He denied it. Said he told Davy "no".' She laughed. 'Told a toddler "no" and he expected him to listen. Can you believe it?'

'How bad is it?' I asked, looking at Davy, who was still sitting and sucking.

She shrugged. 'The stomach pain, the vomiting, the hyperactivity. They're all symptoms. We won't know for a while how much permanent damage there is.'

I was listening with dawning horror. 'LaRoche knew, didn't he?'

Janalee looked at me. 'Knew that Davy had lead poisoning? Yes, I told him. Not that he cared.'

'No, I mean he knew about you and Antonio.' I couldn't stop myself now. The horror of a grown man poisoning a child because he wasn't his own was beyond belief. 'He knew Davy wasn't his baby.'

Janalee acted like she hadn't heard me. She picked up Davy. 'I need to get him home.'

But I wasn't listening to her. I was looking at the spot where Davy had sat. His diaper had leaked and left a perfect oval. Like the one Sarah and I had been trying to cover with the trophy table.

I looked back up at Janalee. She was wiping Davy's mouth with a cloth diaper. The diaper brushed the front of her dark dress, which showed the lint from the cloth the way my own black dress had shown the dog hair. But rather than Frank's long hair, these were tiny white flecks. Flecks like the ones mixed in with the drying blood on my hand after I'd touched the tablecloth.

Janalee was talking baby talk to Davy. 'Daddies take good care of their babies, don't they, Davy? Real daddies don't do things to hurt them.'

She looked up at me. 'Marvin was a coward. He didn't even have the courage to hurt us himself. He let Davy hurt himself. He burned down Janalee's Place to hurt me.' She shook her head slowly back and forth. 'Marvin deserved to die.'

'So you killed him?' At that moment I wanted to give her a trophy for it. Just not *the* trophy.

'I was the one who should have killed him,' Amy said, stepping into the room. 'The night he burned down the store.' She looked at Janalee. '*Our* store.'

I thought of seeing her on the cellphone that night. 'He called and warned you, and you went back there to stop him. But you stopped at Schultz's Market first,' I said, puzzled. 'Why would you do that?'

'To buy a knife.' She walked over to Janalee and gave Davy a kiss on the forehead. 'I didn't have time for anything else.'

'Were you lovers?' I asked.

'Just once,' she said, glancing guiltily over at Janalee. 'I'm so sorry, Janalee.'

'I know,' Janalee said. 'Marvin always wanted what he couldn't have. It was a game for him, I told you. It wasn't your fault.'

That's when it hit me. Amy and Janalee both had been in the competition room. Neither one of them could have placed the table over the body by herself. I'd had to have Sarah help me move it.

'Amy didn't have anything to do with it,' Janalee said, like she was reading my thoughts.

'She must have helped you hide the body. It would have taken two people to move that table.'

'The man was an animal,' Amy exploded. 'He deserved to die.'

In my book he deserved far worse, though I couldn't think of what that would be at the moment. I'd be willing to give it a shot, though.

'So you killed him?' I was looking at Amy, but Janalee answered.

'I said Amy had nothing to do with it.' When the barista started to protest, Janalee waved her down. 'I don't regret what I did.' She looked me in the eye. 'I saved my child.'

'But how? What was LaRoche doing here so late?' I asked. It still didn't make sense to me.

'Marvin planned to sabotage the other competitors' work stations so I would win,' Janalee said. 'He thought that with Amy leaving, it was our only hope of winning.' This last was in a whisper.

'But he didn't know who would compete at which station,' I said. 'I hadn't decided.'

'I told him I knew which station was assigned to me,' she said in a stronger voice. Then she smiled. 'And he believed me.'

LaRoche might have presumed he was the master strategist in the family, but he was wrong. It was Janalee. She had learned how to push Marvin's buttons, and she had pushed this final one in order to lure him into the competition room to kill him.

The question was, what did I do about it?

TWENTY-THREE

IN A PERFECT WORLD, ethics and morals would be the same thing. What our innards tell us is right would be what society also believes is right.

My world wasn't looking very perfect right now. A whole lot more grays than blacks and whites.

I was sitting on the edge of a planter in the front hall of the convention center, watching the roofers move in. I'd left Janalee and Amy in the competition room—mostly, because I hadn't known what to do with them.

I tried to think of Janalee's exact words. She'd alluded to saving her child, but I didn't think she had actually come out and admitted killing her husband. But she had killed LaRoche, I knew that in my heart.

And, God help me, I was glad. The man was a monster. Yes, Janalee had an affair and tried to pass off the product of that affair—Davy—as LaRoche's child. LaRoche had every right to be angry. But to hurt Davy in an effort to punish Janalee? It was unconscionable.

I thought about the pathetic folder marked 'competitive strategies' that Janalee had given me by mistake. I'd assumed it was the sign of an obsessed mother. Little did I know that Janalee had good reason for tracking Davy's health so compulsively.

LaRoche had followed the same strategy when he burned down Janalee's Place. Janalee had loved it, so he destroyed it. With the fire, though, he'd gotten two for the price of one. He'd also been able to punish Amy for seeming to rebuff him for Levitt.

All this, and probably a fat insurance policy on the store, too, assuming they couldn't trace the arson back to him. That was probably why he had accused me—to deflect possible blame. It apparently was his modus operandi.

Two burly men came past with what looked like a huge rolled-up banner balanced on their shoulders. I slid sideways on the wall, so they could back up enough to maneuver through the door and into the exhibit hall.

Janalee and Amy still hadn't come out of the competition room. They were probably wondering what I was going to do. Heck, I was wondering what I was going to do.

I could go to Pavlik and tell him what I knew. Or thought I knew. I really had no proof, after all.

The thought perked me right up. I didn't have any evidence, just unfounded hunches, the kinds of things Pavlik had dismissed time and time again.

The only fingerprints on the trophy were mine, presumably because Janalee had wiped it off with one of the cloth diapers she used as burp cloths. I now knew there was no camera in the back hallway, so Janalee certainly hadn't been caught on that and, as far as I knew, no one else had seen her that night. The only one who could have seen her was me, and I could honestly say I hadn't.

It was like a weight had been lifted off my shoulders. The fact that it was obfuscation and rationalization that had lifted it didn't matter for now. Tonight, when I was awakened at three a.m. by a guilty conscience, maybe it would matter. But that, to paraphrase Scarlett again, was another day.

And I could always tell Pavlik then, if I had a change of heart. Like it hardened.

I stood up, feeling ever so much better. Stepping away from the wall, I was almost mowed down by the same two men who had come through with the banner. Antonio was close behind them and steadied me.

'What are you still doing here?' I asked after I thanked him.

He pointed to a small push cart. 'My guys forgot this, so I am taking it in my car. And you, Maggy? Why are you here as well?'

'I was just talking to Janalee and Amy,' I said. I didn't know how much Antonio knew, but it struck me that he was as much a victim of LaRoche as Janalee was. It was his son, after all, who was poisoned.

'I'm really sorry about Davy's health problems,' I said to Antonio.

His eyes narrowed a bit. 'The baby's health problems?' he asked. 'Has David fallen ill?'

Antonio seemed genuinely concerned about the boy's health. That pretty much confirmed David's parentage, but now I had stepped in it, in an entirely different way. Apparently Janalee hadn't told Antonio about the lead poisoning.

I would have felt guilty about my mistake, but Janalee hadn't said it was a secret. Besides, she was a murderess, so I figured she couldn't get too ticked at me for being a big mouth.

'Davy has lead poisoning,' I said with that big mouth.

Antonio just looked at me, his head tilted.

'Janalee said so.'

He looked even more perplexed.

'Are you OK?' I asked.

'Yes, yes,' Antonio said. 'I just do not understand. David's tests were all perfect.'

'This may have been relatively recently,' I said, thinking Antonio was talking about the Apgar test they administer to newborns.

But Antonio was already shaking his head. 'The tests, they were just last week.'

Now *I* didn't understand. 'What were they for?'

'A medical examination and a test to make certain the…what do you call it? Paternity?'

'You didn't believe that Davy was your son?'

'I did, but she—'

I interrupted. 'Janalee thought that Davy might be LaRoche's son?' Couldn't keep up with the bedmates without a score card, apparently.

'She said she must make sure he had no claim on David,' Antonio said. 'Nor his family.'

'Was she planning on leaving LaRoche and marrying you?' I asked.

'Marrying?' He looked horrified at the thought. 'No, Maggy, you do not understand. I merely provided the sperm.'

But… 'Why didn't LaRoche provide the sperm?'

'Because he did not want a baby. When Janalee asked him, he said he would get snipped.' He made a scissors gesture with his fingers.

Ouch. But I needed to get this straight. 'So, Janalee wanted a baby. LaRoche, knowing that, threatened to get a vasectomy.'

Antonio nodded.

'So why was he crying after you and he fought?'

'We argued about his speech, not David. I was angry because he had acted as my friend, sharing information about his business. So I, in turn, shared information about my business, The Milkman.'

'And he used that information to set himself up to compete with you,' I said, understanding. 'That's exactly what he did with us.'

'Yes.' Antonio was nodding. 'He said it was a battle he was fighting on many...how you say? Fronts?'

I nodded. I wasn't sure anything I heard about La-Roche would surprise me anymore.

'I was angry. He was angry,' Antonio continued. 'But I do not see him crying. He's a man, after all.'

I'd debate that at this point.

Antonio was holding up a finger. 'He did sneeze. The hay fever perhaps?'

What did Pavlik say? The simplest solution is usually the right one? So much less satisfying than LaRoche crying, but I'd have to settle for it. 'So you donated your sperm, and Janalee got pregnant.'

'Immediately,' Antonio said proudly.

'Immediately,' I echoed. 'And we know that Davy is your baby because Janalee had you take a paternity test. And that she didn't want LaRoche or his family to have any claim on Davy.'

'Yes.' Antonio didn't seem to see why I found this so confusing.

The fact that Janalee wanted the test meant she was planning to leave LaRoche and didn't want a custody fight. Or...

'And you are absolutely certain that Davy was healthy when blood was taken for the test?' I asked.

Antonio nodded one last time. *'Absolutamente.'*

Well, I'll be.

The bitch had completely snowed me, and I'd almost let her walk.

Leaving Antonio behind, I ran through the exhibit hall to the door of the competition room. Janalee and Amy were still there. Janalee was changing Davy's diaper.

'Janalee!' I yelled, thereby joining every fictional character I've ever disparaged for giving the bad guy warning before grabbing them.

She turned.

'You lied to me.' I advanced on her. 'Davy is not sick.'

Janalee picked up Davy, bare bottom and all.

Amy got between us. 'That's just not true, Maggy. He has lead poisoning and Marvin—'

'Oh, cut the bullshit, Amy,' I said. 'Either you're in on this, too, or you're as stupid as I am.' Or was.

My anger level surprised me. Now that 'moral' and 'ethical' were synonymous again, my world was back in balance and, apparently, there was no stopping me. I wasn't sure if that was a good thing or not.

'Why would Janalee make this up?' Amy asked, holding up her hands. I could see Janalee edging toward the side door.

'Because she got caught,' I said. 'She figured that I would fall for her sob story and keep my mouth shut.'

And she had almost figured right. She had manipulated me just like she'd manipulated LaRoche to lure him into the competition room. She had used our weaknesses—and our strengths—against us.

'Know your enemy', Sun Tzu's *The Art of War,* had preached. LaRoche had been a disciple of Sun Tzu, and Janalee had taken a page out of her husband's own book and used it against him. And me. Janalee had known exactly how to gain my sympathy.

I feared that said something about me—something bad, but I'd have to sort that out later. For now, I was going to take Janalee down.

'Don't be silly, Maggy.' Amy said, still blocking my way. 'Janalee told me about Davy's…' She hesitated. 'Problem, days ago.'

'Davy's only problem is a crazy mom and an upset stomach,' I said. 'And I'm willing to bet that she told you when she needed you to do something, just like she did me. Maybe when she wanted help to cover up the body or…'

I left off. Things were all falling into place.

Still backing up, Janalee met my eyes defiantly.

'Or,' I continued, 'when she called to tell you Marvin was going to burn down the store.'

I turned back to Amy. 'It was Janalee on the phone with you outside Schultz's Market, wasn't it? That's why you were crying. She was telling you about Davy.'

Amy was shaking now, her earrings making the same tinkling sound they had as we'd stood on the stage over LaRoche's body.

'He was destroying everything,' she said. 'First Davy, then Janalee's Place. She said I had to stop him, because she wasn't strong enough. I thought—' she looked over at Janalee— 'I thought I owed it to her because of what I'd done.'

A one-night stand with a snake. There was something biblical about that. 'So you bought a knife,' I said, 'and went to Janalee's Place.'

'It was too late,' Amy whispered hoarsely. 'When I got there, the store was already burning, and Marvin was gone.'

'Because he was never there,' I said. 'Right, Janalee?'

The woman didn't answer. She was holding Davy tight against her. I was afraid she would smother him.

'Give me David,' I said, moving toward her. Janalee threw me a startled look.

'You set the fire?' Amy asked her incredulously. 'You burned down the Place?'

'I had to get away from him,' Janalee said. Her face was nearly unrecognizable. 'In order to keep Davy and the rest of the coffeehouses, I had to sacrifice Janalee's Place.'

'And me, Janalee? Did you have to sacrifice me, too?'

Amy's words hung in the air for a beat.

Then Janalee took off running.

'You go out front to cut her off,' I yelled at Amy and followed Janalee out into the side corridor. 'Whatever you do, don't let her get in the exhibit hall.'

Encumbered by Davy, Janalee hadn't gotten very far, just to the entrance of the bar that Kate, Jerome and I had visited the night of the murder. Davy was screaming now, so I knew he was still breathing, at least.

Janalee hesitated, apparently not sure whether to take a shortcut through the bar or continue down the hall. She glanced in and made her decision.

Hall, it was, and I was on her heels. I'd been afraid she'd opt to go through the bar, but when I got there, I realized why she hadn't. The place was filled with roofers, priming themselves for the convention.

Also in the bar, seated at a table near the door, were Kate and Jerome finishing up lunch. I saw Kate's head follow Janalee, then she glanced back and registered my presence.

'She killed LaRoche,' I shouted as I passed.

'Grab your camera, Jack,' I heard Kate tell Jerome.

Reinforcements—or at least documentation—were on their way. I continued my chase.

Janalee had reached the door that led into the Grand Foyer of the convention center. She glanced over her shoulder at me, just feet behind her, and then shoved on the push bar.

The door opened and released us into the big entry hall. Where the bar had been full, the Grand Foyer was empty. Apparently everyone had finished their set-ups and broken for a late lunch before the attendees came in. The registration table stood ready, but was unattended.

No help was to be found inside and I was losing steam. Shouldn't have given up those morning aerobics classes in favor of work. And sleep.

There was only one thing to do.

I slowed down and Janalee, thinking she was home free, made for the big revolving door. Once in the bay, she pushed hard. The door went whirling, Janalee and Davy in it.

'Stop her,' I screamed, forced to wait for the thing to slow down so I could get into it. I had to time it like I was dashing into a game of jump rope. One, two, three, GO!

I made the plunge, but Janalee and Davy had already been propelled out the other side. I emerged just in time to see Janalee and two roofers scrambling to their feet on the other side. But where was Davy?

'I have him,' a voice to my right said. 'And it's a damned good thing I quit smoking, or I would have had a cigarette in my hand when they came shooting out that door. Just managed to grab the kid before Janalee went down.'

Sarah was holding the bare-bottomed baby carefully away from her body. 'Why's he naked?' she asked.

I knew that as long as we had Davy, Janalee wouldn't take off. Not that I was stupid enough to chance it.

'Grab her,' I said to the roofers. 'She's a murderer.'

Roofers being good sports, they obliged. I looked around. Kate and Jerome were already there taping. They must have gone outside through the bar and come around to catch the action out front.

Besides the two of them, there were seven men and women, all smoking cigarettes. Different day, different convention, different people, but you could always count on the smokers' circle.

And Sarah.

TWENTY-FOUR

BY THE TIME AMY AND Antonio arrived, the police were on their way.

'I'm sorry,' Amy said breathlessly. 'I was going out to stop her like you said.' She looked over at Janalee, who was ringed by roofers. 'But I banged right into Antonio.'

'I did not know why you had run away when we were talking,' Antonio explained, turning to me. 'I was concerned.'

'I tried to tell him about Janalee and Marvin and the table and…me…' Amy was tearing up.

Antonio took up the story. 'She began crying as she is now, so I could not understand a word she said. When she finally composed herself—'

'Is Davy safe?' Amy interrupted.

I turned in the direction she was looking. Sarah had handed the baby to one of the roofers. As we watched, she shrugged out of her baggy jacket and wrapped the baby in it.

'Strangely enough,' I said, smiling, 'I think he's just fine.'

'WHAT WILL HAPPEN to Davy?' I asked Pavlik. We were sitting on the steps of my porch. Pavlik was throwing the ball for Frank.

'For now, he's with Antonio,' he said, wiping slobber off his throwing hand. 'He's the father, with the paternity tests to prove it.'

I shook my head. 'I'm not so sure Antonio is prepared to be a father. You should have seen his reaction to the word 'marriage'.'

Pavlik looked sideways at me. 'We all have that reaction. Some of us are just better at hiding it than others.'

I laughed. 'Thanks,' I said. 'I'll remember that should I ever have those kind of thoughts about you.'

'Don't get me wrong,' he continued. 'The right woman could make any man want to settle down.'

I sensed a moment of danger. I didn't know if I was afraid of scaring him off, or I was afraid of scaring *me* off. Either way, my reply was the same.

'I don't want to "settle down",' I said, making the quotation marks with my fingers. 'Been there, done that.'

'Me, too,' he said cheerfully, thereby dashing my hopes that he would be inconsolable. 'But maybe Amy is the kind of woman to get Antonio to settle down.'

'Amy, huh?' I wasn't quite seeing it. 'They seem like polar opposites,' I protested. 'Amy is heavy metal, Antonio is flamenco.'

'Yes, but it's all just music, isn't it?'

'A philosopher,' I said, elbowing him. 'I'm impressed.'

'Not yet,' he said, kissing me lightly on the lips. 'But you will be.'

'Not still mad at me for confronting Janalee instead of coming to you?' I asked. He'd been a bit cranky about that when he'd arrived on the scene.

'I got over it.'

Good thing neither of us held grudges. I had a feeling that might come in handy. 'Wine?' I asked.

'Sure,' Pavlik said. 'Want me to get it?'

'Nah.' I stood up. 'You create a diversion, so Frank doesn't follow me in.'

Frank gave me a suspicious look. He knew I was talking about him, not that he cared. The sheepdog dropped the tennis ball in Pavlik's lap and backed up, waiting for the throw.

'Diversion created,' Pavlik said.

'Yeah.' I opened the door and went in, unimpeded. Apparently I was one rung below Pavlik on the sheepdog's hierarchal ladder.

Opening the refrigerator, I pulled out the Fumé Blanc I'd put in to chill.

'White wine?' Pavlik said, when I handed him a glass. 'I thought you always drank red.'

'It's an unseasonably warm Fall day,' I said, settling down next to him. 'I thought white would be nice.'

I took a sip. Nice, but no Pinot Noir. I put the glass where Frank couldn't knock it over. 'Besides, it's not healthy to get in a rut. Before you know it, the rut becomes an addiction.'

'Addiction?' Pavlik was studying my face.

'Or maybe an obsession.' I leaned back against the step. 'Jerome says his father has a theory. He says we're all addicted to something, and that's not necessarily bad. The trick is to make sure they are *good* things.'

'Red wine is supposed to be good for you,' Pavlik reminded me.

'As is dark chocolate, my other guilty pleasure.' I picked up the ball Frank had dropped in front of Pavlik and threw it. 'Thing is, it probably wouldn't hurt for me to cut down on both of them.'

Pavlik swirled the wine in his glass. 'So you're going to switch to white wine?'

'And milk chocolate,' I said ruefully. 'I don't like either of them very much, so I figure I'll naturally cut down on my consumption of both. I think of it as my answer to Sarah's nicotine inhaler.'

Pavlik laughed. 'Let's hope it's more effective. I heard her asking one of the guys for a smoke as we were leaving.'

'Not for *a* smoke,' I said. 'She was asking him *to* smoke. Sarah's into second-hand smoke.'

Pavlik just looked at me.

'She's weaning herself,' I said. 'What can I say?'

The sheriff shook his head, and set his glass down next to mine. Apparently he didn't like white much, either. 'So Sarah's addicted to cigarettes. You, it's red wine and dark chocolate.'

'Then there's LaRoche.' I'd been giving this a lot of thought. 'His was power. He needed to control—to maneuver people like he did his toy soldiers.'

'I wonder who gets custody of the soldiers.' Pavlik looked more concerned about the soldiers than he had about Davy.

'Janalee, on the other hand,' I continued, ignoring him, 'lives for her child. That's what you would call a good addiction, I guess.'

'Until you murder someone,' Pavlik said dryly.

Yeah, there was that.

'Let's see. Who else?' Pavlik was getting into the swing of things. 'Levitt and Amy—alcohol, of course.'

I threw him a startled look.

'What?' he said. 'You seriously thought I didn't know? I *am* the sheriff, after all.' He patted himself on the chest.

I shook my head. 'OK, wise guy. If you know so much, tell me why you said Antonio and Amy could become a couple.'

I liked the thought of the two of them raising Davy— or David, as Antonio called him—and living happily every after. I'm a sucker for a happy ending.

'Stranger things have happened,' Pavlik said, wrestling the ball away from Frank. 'Though I have to say I'm a little confused about Amy and Janalee's relationship.'

'I know. But like Antonio said—' I affected his accent— '"A casual friendship, a great love—who are we on the outside to know?"'

'Horrible Italian accent,' Pavlik said, 'but I get your point.'

'Besides, I don't think things are as clear cut as they were when we were young,' I said, settling back against the step. 'Eric says that kids are exploring their sexuality more these days. Gay, straight, bi-sexual—whatever.'

Pavlik was teasing the dog, now, pretending to throw the ball. 'I'm probably engaging in a little wishful thinking, anyway, about those two.'

'Which two? Amy and Janalee, or Amy and Antonio?'

'The latter.' Pavlik faked another toss and hid the ball behind me on the step.

'You don't want Amy to be gay?' I asked, trying to push the slimy ball away from me.

'I don't want Antonio to be available.' He turned toward me. 'You seem to find him altogether too charming.'

'He,' I said, pulling the tennis ball out from behind my now drool-stained back, 'doesn't slime me.'

'I could be charming *and* slime you. Try me.' Pavlik leaned down to kiss me.

'And how about you, Sheriff?' I said afterwards, a little breathlessly. 'What's your addiction?'

'My addiction?' He was looking into my eyes. 'I think you—'

WHUMP! Frank had found the tennis ball.

In an effort to get to it, the dog landed on Pavlik. Pavlik, in turn, fell on top of me, pinning me to the steps.

A sheepdog and sheriff sandwich.

I was just *never* going to have sex.

* * * * *